DEATH RETIRES

A DEATH RETIRED MYSTERY

CATE LAWLEY

ALSO BY CATE LAWLEY

VEGAN VAMP MYSTERIES

Adventures of a Vegan Vamp

The Client's Conundrum

The Elvis Enigma

The Nefarious Necklace

The Halloween Haunting

The Selection Shenanigans

The Cupid Caper

The Reluctant Renfield

NIGHT SHIFT WITCH MYSTERIES

Night Shift Witch

Star of the Party

Tickle the Dragon's Tail

Twinkles Takes a Holiday

DEATH RETIRED

Death Retires

A Date with Death

On the Street Where Death Lives

With a Little Bit of Death

FAIRMONT FINDS CANINE COZY MYSTERIES

On the Trail of a Killer

The Scent of a Poet's Past

Sniffing Out Sweet Secrets

Tracking a Poison Pen

CURSED CANDY MYSTERIES

Cutthroat Cupcakes

Twisted Treats

Fatal Fudge

Tea with a Demon: A Cursed Candy Short

Brunch with a Scurry of Squirrels: A Cursed Candy Short

LOVE EVER AFTER

Heartache in Heels

Skeptic in a Skirt

Pretty in Peep-Toes

Love Ever After Boxed Set One

LUCKY MAGIC

Lucky Magic

Luck of the Devil

Luck of the Draw

Wicked Bad Luck

For the most current listing of Cate's books, visit her website:

www.CateLawley.com

Sunday morning, late August

"Hello!" The feminine voice was attached to an even more womanly figure approaching from across the street.

My new four-foot, rose-draped fence seemed woefully inadequate as I crouched behind it.

"Mr. Todd!"

I lowered my head and busied myself removing the dried petals of the dead flower. Pinching away, I tried to remember the name as my curvy neighbor approached. Red cascade. The realtor had said when I'd viewed the house.

The previous owners had trained the stems upward and the bloom-filled vines now flowed down the square-mesh fencing. But they didn't flow quite enough, because she, the woman of the curves, kept calling.

"Yoo-hoo! Mr. Todd!"

A flash of bright pink peeked through the vines. My thorny wall had too many holes.

"Mr. Todd?" she called again, closer now.

A weedy patch caught my eye, and I turned my attention to yanking the stubborn intruders out by the root. As I worked at the soil, I considered my fencing predicament. Perhaps a ten-foot, solid-metal fence sent the wrong message to the neighbors. Perhaps I didn't care.

"Hi!" the woman called from much, much too close. I could even smell her over the scent of freshly-turned earth. She had a baked-cookie scent that made my mouth water.

Looking up, I found my neighbor peering down at me from across the fence. With her pink sundress and her dark hair all twisted up, I couldn't tell if she'd spent five minutes on her toilette or an hour. Naturally gorgeous or made up to look it, I didn't know. Didn't want to know.

That's her. She's the one. Hey, buddy, that's her!

The voice in my head I could ignore, but with the woman looking right at me, it would be more difficult.

"Morning." Against all my inclinations, I didn't stand, clinging to some hope that my rudeness would shorten the interaction. People were difficult, and I needed a little more practice before I jumped fully into the world of small talk and social repartee.

"I'm Sylvie Baker, your neighbor." She gave me an expectant smile. When I remained silent, she pointed to a house kitty-corner to mine. "Just there. That's me."

Of course it was. I already knew that, because the persistent voice in my head had told me as much.

The neighborhood was gentrifying—short-term renters were giving way to owners—and some of my new neighbors were interested in building a "community." I'd known that when I bought the house—and I'd bought it anyway.

If I'd known about the house kitty-corner and it's occupant, I might have reconsidered.

"Geoff Todd. Just moved in." I remained firmly crouched behind my fence.

She didn't take the hint. Worse, she smiled brightly. "I know. It's a small, chatty neighborhood, and we like to keep each other up-to-date. It's nice to meet you, Geoff."

And like that, we were on a first-name basis.

Geoffy. Geoffy-Geoffy-Geoff.

I ignored the singsong voice and turned back to my stubborn weed. With a vicious yank, it came loose and I chucked it over my shoulder.

Unfortunately, my behavior didn't dissuade Sylvie Baker one iota. She just leaned on the fence rail, mindful of the thorns, and asked, "What brings you to the neighborhood, Geoff? Are you new to Austin?"

"No, I retired recently. Wanted to downsize."

"Well, aren't you the lucky one." She flashed another smile, this time revealing a fetching dimple. "And young enough to enjoy it."

Since I was starting to ache from all the avoidance weeding, I stood up. My right knee caught for a split second and then let out a loud pop. That was something I'd have to get used to.

The few remaining weeds beckoned. I considered them, then my knees, then glanced up to see if she'd taken the hint and left.

No, still here.

Eye contact was a mistake, because Sylvie immediately let loose with her next volley. "What was your profession? Before you retired, I mean. I do hair." Her eyes narrowed. "I'd be happy to give you a discount. You could do with a trim."

My eyebrows climbed. "Could I?"

"Unless you're going for that disheveled, absent-minded professor look." Her brown eyes assessed my stubbly cheeks, faded jeans, and dark T-shirt in one sweeping glance. "You've got that down."

Since I didn't know that was a look or whether it was a desirable one, I refrained from comment.

"What was it you said you did before you retired?"

I hadn't said. When filling out my retirement packet, I'd gone with what I'd deemed an innocuous profession. Within days, I'd acquired a new past, manufactured to spec. One I'd spent a good amount of time learning. "Teacher. I was a teacher."

Liar, liar, pants on fire.

I ignored the voice.

"A retired teacher." She flashed me that dimpled smile again, like I'd said something both amusing and worthy. "I'm so glad that you've joined the neighborhood, Geoff. Welcome."

An uneasy feeling grabbed me right in the gut. The house had felt right, and the quiet neighborhood had felt welcoming on a level I hadn't understood nor bothered to plumb. But now, with an inescapable voice in my head and my persistent, mouthwatering neighbor standing so near, I couldn't help questioning whether settling into this particular corner of Austin had been the best choice.

Teacher? You? Liar, liar. Shame.

Perhaps questioning the choice was too mild. I was doubting my sanity, both in making this choice and in choosing to stay.

"Ah, thanks." I paused, then added, "Sylvie."

The voice howled victoriously in my ear.

G eoff. Geoffy-Geoff. You have ears. You hear me.
"You need to get rid of that guy. He's seriously cramping my style." The bobcat's mouth didn't move, but the voice was his.

Unlike the ghosts that whispered in my ear—including the one in my living room right now who was taunting me— anyone could hear Clarence. A problem, because he wasn't the most discreet of creatures, and he happened to be my responsibility.

"What style is our visiting ghost cramping?" I asked.

He stretched, his huge paws pushed straight out in front of him and his bobtailed bottom high in the air. Then he flopped over on his side, diving cheek first. Once he was comfortably situated, he lifted his back leg in the air and—

"Stop. You know the rules: no cleaning your business in mixed company."

Clarence grumbled.

"What were you saying about style?" I redirected him to his previous rant in hopes of avoiding the you'd-do-it-if-you-could-reach-it speech.

Sprawling, but more circumspectly now, he said, "That ghost has to go." Except he didn't sound that concerned, and he certainly didn't answer my question.

Boo!

I ignored the voice. That strategy hadn't proven successful thus far, but until I had other alternatives I was sticking to it.

"You do recognize that you're a shade away from being a ghost yourself, Clarence. I'm surprised you don't have more sympathy."

He sneezed.

When he was done spreading cat snot all over my stained concrete floor, he said, "A shade, that's cute. But let me ask you this: am I corporeal?" He didn't wait for a response. His whiskers twitched, then he said, "If I have a body, I'm not a ghost. Simple math, bozo."

I crossed my arms. "Your ghostly self stole that body and, if I had to guess, got stuck."

Not that I knew. No one knew how Clarence had ended as he had, a human ghost in the physical body of a wildcat. Or no one was sharing that information with me.

He rolled around on my bobcat-snot-covered floors, trying to scratch his back.

He seemed happy enough, so I was hardly certain he'd been stuck. Maybe he stayed by choice.

"Quit it." I snatched a tuft of hair floating through the air. "You're getting hair everywhere and stinking up the place."

He purred. "You know you love it."

He smelled not unpleasantly of the outdoors, a pine-forested version, and not like a nasty, musky wildcat, so he wasn't entirely wrong. But it was disturbing to see him wallow on my floor in feline ecstasy. Maybe if I didn't know he was human . . . No, it was unsettling either way.

"You've got to stop that."

He flopped over on his side again and let loose another sneeze. "Man, these allergies are killing me. Can you find out if I can take Zyrtec in this body? I don't know if it's the mold or the pollen or the—"

"You don't need allergy medication. You need to stop rolling in every stray weed patch you come across."

"Just a quick pharmacy run. I can check online if cats can take—" His eyes widened, eyeing the newspaper I'd retrieved from the coffee table.

I started to roll it. "You were saying?"

A nasty feline growl emerged from deep in his chest. "Nothing." With a sniff, he added, "Forget the drugs."

The idea of corporal punishment made me squirm, but if Clarence thought the threat was real, I'd use it—the threat, not the newspaper. I tossed the paper back onto the coffee table.

After a few seconds of much too short, blissful silence, he said, "It's past time to get rid of the ghost. You know, he might go away if you did what he wanted."

I choked out a negative response. Clarence *would* think that.

Kitty, kitty, kitty. Here, kitty.

My left eye started to twitch.

Maybe Clarence could hear our ghostly visitor because he was still technically a ghost himself—a ghost permanently possessing a twenty-five-pound bobcat, perhaps, but still a ghost. He could hear and see ghosts better than I could, and he didn't get twitchy or headachy from their presence. Unlike Clarence, I could only see them when they wanted to be seen.

Kitty, kitty.

Or hear them when they wanted to be heard.

The constant interruptions from this particular disembodied voice had begun to make my left eye twitch.

Ghosts were a pestilence upon the planet. It was a good thing most of them didn't have much shelf life.

Unfortunately, the one that kept hassling Clarence and me seemed to be fresh. He was also grounded close by—kitty-corner to my home, to be exact—so he could recharge and return to hassle us multiple times a day.

He was becoming a nuisance. No. He'd *been* a nuisance when I discovered him lurking the second day after I moved in. What he'd become in the intervening week was an eye-twitching headache. And if he stayed much longer, I suspected he'd be a deep, throbbing, icepick-to-my-eye migraine.

"You know, Clarence, you're right."

"Huh?" He lifted his chin from the floor and gave me a suspicious look.

"We're going to do something about our uninvited houseguest."

Suspicion turned to discontent, and he gave me his best bobcat kitty glare. "Whoa, whoa, whoa. *We* are? You're the one who should be doing something. You're the big D, so he's your problem. But, uh, maybe hold off on the scary death stare till you know what he really wants."

Now that was intriguing. Clarence had thus far been lukewarm *against* the ghost. The shift had me questioning his motives.

"I'm not the 'big D.' I'm retired." I settled into my favorite armchair. "And there's no such thing as a death stare. Although if there were, I'd love to use it on whoever botched this ghost's collection."

When souls were separated cleanly, collected, and moved on to wherever they were going, ghosts didn't happen. That was my theory, anyway. And since I'd been death—more accurately, one of the deaths—for several decades, I probably had a better handle on what made ghosts than most people.

"Uh-huh. Sure, big D. There's no death stare, just like retired soul collectors can't hear ghosts."

The second part was true, until me. Or none of the other retirees were fessing up to the ability because they wanted to lounge in peaceful obscurity, hidden away from needy specters.

As death, seeing ghosts came in handy. As a retired "teacher," it was not convenient.

Geooooof. Oh, Geoffy-boy. Pretty lady, across the street. So preeeetty.

Damned *in*convenient, in fact. Time to start searching for exorcism rituals.

If there were ghosts, then there must be ways to get rid of ghosts.

It was only logical.

Sunday afternoon

"Ghost removal? I can't help you." Lilac, a medium I'd discovered in the yellow pages, wasn't quite living up to my expectations. Younger, prettier, greener, and more pierced than I'd expected—but also not nearly as cooperative as I'd hoped.

Then again, the yellow pages weren't cutting-edge advertising any longer, per Clarence. I'd had my suspicions. I had been living in and around people the last few decades—just not *as* a person—but old habits liked to cling. In the world I'd known, there'd been phone books and people had used them.

Lilac's gaze shifted to Clarence. "What exactly does an emotional support cat do?"

"Ah . . ." I glared at Clarence. He'd told me to say that. Had sworn it would get him in the door, no questions asked, and since he'd threatened to spray my bed if I didn't take him along, I'd conceded.

Lilac waved a heavily ringed hand. "Never mind." Her words might have been dismissive, but she wouldn't stop looking at me as if I had something in between my teeth. "You're sure your place is haunted? I can come out and do a preliminary screening for a modest fee. Just to double-check it's not, you know, something else. Something not other-worldly."

Ah. The medium thought I was nuts.

When the woman with the fluorescent, green hair, bright blue nail polish, and five competing spiritual philosophies plastered on her walls thought I was delusional, I might need to consider how I was presenting myself to the public.

Or stop taking Clarence's advice. I turned a critical eye on my four-legged companion.

The leash pulled tight as Clarence tried to run for the hills, or at least for the safety of the small space under Lilac's couch.

Twenty-five pounds of cat was a lot of feline, but a long way from being able to yank me around. I planted my feet and let him struggle. We'd already had one harness-slipping incident, so I'd made darn sure the thing was snug this time.

"I think something's upset your cat." Lilac's eyebrows, thankfully not green, rose as she watched Clarence's paws slip and slide on her laminate flooring.

"He's fine." Though I did grip the leash tighter. "Thanks for your offer, but the voices I'm hearing are very real. I had a colleague verify the ghost's presence."

Clarence must have been mollified by my "colleague" reference, because he stopped pulling. A split second later, he was flopped on the ground and had assumed the pose of a serenely relaxed cat. That lasted just long enough for him to shoot me a taunting glance, then he kicked a back leg high in the air and started to clean *all* his parts.

Gritting my teeth, I turned back to the lovely and less-than-helpful Lilac. "There has to be a way to get rid of a ghost. Every pest has a weakness."

Lilac narrowed her eyes. "I wouldn't exactly call a spirit visiting from another plane of existence a pest."

"And that tells me you're not living with one." I closed my eyes and did a quick mental reset. When I opened them, I smiled with as much warmth as I could muster. That used to work well with women—several decades ago, when I'd been human. "I'm sorry. I'm frustrated, and that's not your fault. Do you have any recommendations for me?"

Her eyes went wide, and she stared for a few seconds. When she did finally blink, it looked like she was fighting her way through a dust storm.

Looked like I might have lost the knack for charming women. That or modern women found a little focused attention terrifying. I waited for her to get her bearings again.

Eventually, she frowned at me and then Clarence. "You could try asking your ghost what he wants."

Clarence coughed and then started to hack as if a monstrous hairball were caught in his throat. Except that was no hairball.

I watched him laugh maniacally for a few more seconds, and when it looked like he wasn't stopping anytime soon, I raised my voice. "I know what he wants."

She tipped her head inquisitively as Clarence continued to cackle like a demented crow.

Clarence fell silent just as the tail end of my response boomed through the room. "He wants me to have sex with his wife."

Sunday evening

Awkward. That summed up the remainder of my session with Lilac, the green-haired medium.

Things hadn't changed that much with women over the years. Add sex to the mix and everything went topsy-turvy.

I tried to explain that it was our resident ghost who was the pervert and not me, but that hadn't gone to plan. I finally opted to retreat when it became clear the situation had devolved beyond recovery. I scheduled a second session before I was shown the door, but I suspected it would be chaperoned by a very large friend.

If she thought I was a lunatic, so be it, so long as she didn't try to get me committed. Four white walls would drive me nuttier than the ghostly voices. But I was willing to risk a second meeting, because I'd sniffed a whiff of real talent underneath the green hair and woo-woo façade. There weren't *that* many authentic talents running around in the world. With a little cooperation from Clarence, I planned to discover how much of a medium Lilac really was.

An unexpected positive result had been the ease of the interaction, except for that part at the end. I'd found the shop, introduced myself, and even started to have a reasonable conversation about a desired service. I hadn't done too terribly, emotional support cat aside. It had been . . . not horrible.

Lilac had voiced subtle concerns about my sanity, but that hadn't happened until the very end. Even as badly as it ended, I'd survived with nothing more than a few embarrassing memories. Perhaps I'd been too hasty in my attempted brush-off of the friendly Sylvie Baker.

My thoughts were interrupted by Clarence's hacking laugh. I glanced in my rearview mirror to check on him.

This time he wasn't laughing, and I had a nasty hairball to clean up when I got home.

"Ugh, that's disgusting. Why my leather seats? Couldn't you keep that mess in your seat?"

He shot me a little side-eye as he coughed one last time. "No. If you're going to make me ride in a booster seat like a kid, then I'm puking on your leather seats. Besides"—he rubbed his jaw along the edge of the cushioned carrier—"this is mine now. Who pukes in their own bed?"

I'd learned quickly that having a loose bobcat in the car, even one possessed by a dead man, was not a good idea. After two near-miss accidents when he'd crawled over me to get a better look out my window, I'd set up some travel rules. One of those rules being that Clarence was only allowed in my car if he was buckled into the booster-seat-like carrier I'd bought for him. He claimed he found it demeaning, but it looked like it was growing on him.

"We gonna ask Bobby why he wants you getting down and dirty with his old lady?" Clarence asked in a studiously nonchalant tone.

"Bobby?" I checked my rearview mirror, but Clarence

wouldn't look me in the eye. I knew there'd been something suspicious going on. "You've been chatting with our ghost?"

No wonder the guy was sticking around. With my house-mate egging him on, he probably thought he had a chance of catching my ear.

"Maybe." Clarence cleared his throat. "You gonna make me eat that crap cat kibble if I say yes?"

My relationship with Clarence consisted of a series of negotiations, bribes, and compromises, with me doing most of the compromising and bribing and Clarence mostly threatening me with bobcat urine and hairballs placed in strategically unpleasant places. I only threatened to bop him on his kitty nose when I'd lost all patience.

Once he'd squirmed enough to make me feel a little less peeved about the hairball cleanup in my near future, I said, "No, not yet. But you—you'll lose fresh-meat privileges if you don't fess up now. And in Clarence speak, that means telling me everything, leaving nothing out that I might consider important."

"Can it wait till we get home? The smell of cat yak is making my stomach turn."

Teeth gritted, I cracked his window and stepped on the gas. Felicide was sadly out of the question. Death of the cat's body was unlikely to have any effect on Clarence other than leaving him without a physical presence. The real loser in that scenario was an innocent animal.

The point was moot, because I was vehemently opposed to physical violence against helpless animals—which was exactly what that bobcat was when Clarence was removed from the equation. I tried not to think about that poor animal, trapped inside its body without any control of its own actions. That just made me angry as hell, which didn't help the situation.

Clarence was an unanswered question on many levels. He

didn't have the same expiration problem that most ghosts had. It was known to happen in some instances. I didn't know why, just that some ghosts—like Clarence—persisted, but most did not. An even more intriguing question was his possession of a nonhuman body. A human ghost inhabiting a nonhuman body hadn't occurred within my experience, and possession shouldn't be possible for extended periods of time. The bobcat was Clarence's permanent host. Mind boggling.

Clarence was an enigma.

An odor rolled through the car, and it wasn't hairball funk. "Ugh, what is that foul stench?" Then I realized what I'd said and clarified, "That fouler stench."

Clarence smirked at me in the mirror. "Yesterday's fish. Better out than in, right?"

A hairball-puking, air-polluting enigma who'd thieved a bobcat's body. And he was all mine to care for, supervise, and prevent from harming others. Joy.

"In answer to your question, no, it is not 'better out than in' when it smells like that." I cracked the remaining windows and mentally scratched fish off the grocery list. "And I will not wait till we're home to hear about you and Bobby."

After some grumping and growling, he relented. "He's good company. Better than *some* people. We watch . . ." Clarence muttered something unintelligible.

"What was that?" But I already knew the answer. Clarence thought he was sneaky, but I'd found him out last week. When he hesitated, I said, "No liver for three days."

"Okay! Give a guy a break. Who knew Geoffy boy was into torture? No liver, humph." He sniffed. "We like to watch *The Great British Baking Show* together. There. Are you happy?"

I couldn't help it; a chuckle slipped out. "I already knew. I just wanted to hear you admit to wanting to watch something besides pornography."

"What? How? Oh, it was that late night binge last week, wasn't it? I knew doing the overnight marathon was a risk, but it was too good a chance to miss." He sniffed again, and I hoped he wasn't about to spray cat snot on my leather seats just because he was a little embarrassed. "It's a good show. And there are hot babes."

"I haven't seen it." Not entirely true, but I wasn't about to make him feel any better. "So, about Bobby?"

"He was a mechanic, died about three weeks ago, and has been haunting his old lady—and us—ever since."

Sylvie Baker hadn't looked like a recent widow in the throes of grief, but one could never tell.

"And why would a dead man want a stranger to sleep with his wife?" I asked.

"Well . . . that's a little complicated."

My trouble radar, finely honed after years spent interacting with the dead, the dying, and the people surrounding them, was pinging like mad. "Spill, Clarence."

"Bobby might have been involved in some unsavory dealings before his death—perhaps dealings that led to his death."

"Perhaps?"

"He's not certain. Death fugue and all that."

It happened, usually when the deceased had died in an especially traumatic way. "Okay, so he doesn't remember his death, probably because he was murdered. That doesn't explain why he wants me to do the horizontal tango with his wife."

Clarence snickered. "Watch it, Geoff. You're dating yourself. Horizontal tango." A snort and a chuckle later, he said, "Sylvie's his ex. They've been divorced a few years, but she was his 'one.' You know, the one who steals your heart. The one you never get over. The one—"

"I understand, Clarence."

"Right. Anyway, he's worried that the people who killed him will come after her next."

"That doesn't explain the sex part." I wasn't risking another euphemism. Some parts of modern life were a piece of cake, but others . . . well, others came a little slower. But I was retired. I had time to fit in.

Who was I kidding? I hadn't fit in back when I was human the first time. What were my chances now?

"Yeah, uh, you know, Bobby's not quite all there."

The singsong voice, the taunts, the childish behavior—no, he wasn't. But Clarence was being shady, even for him, and my radar dinged and flashed neon signs of trouble. I sped up as we approached a speed bump.

Clarence lurched in his carrier as I hit it a hair too fast.

"Watch it," Clarence called out.

"Hm. How about you get around to telling me the important parts, the ones you're leaving out?" I glanced in the mirror and found him staring mulishly back. "Or I can take a few laps around the block and hit every bump at cat-puking speed. I've already got one mess to clean up . . ."

"For a straight and narrow guy, you sure do like your torture. Wait," he said as we approached the turn to our house.

I slowed down.

"Okay, Bobby's convinced if Sylvie rocks your world in the sack, you'll be invested enough to make sure the bad guys don't get her. So turn already. One upchuck session per ride is enough, thanks."

"I wonder what gave him the idea that sex with his ex would guarantee my cooperation?" But I turned, foregoing the speed bumps. My back wouldn't appreciate it any more than Clarence's stomach.

One decidedly guilty-looking bobcat stared out the

window the last few blocks, his nose occasionally twitching at some passing scent.

Finally, I prompted him, "Why?"

"Seriously? Can you blame me? You need to get laid. It's unnatural going all that time without some warm p—"

"Eh-eh. No you don't. Remember the house rules."

A gravelly growl emerged from the backseat. "Only use the second best guest toilet, always flush, don't scare the cleaning lady, and never talk about your sex life, especially in crass and unsavory terms."

"That's right. Do we need to have another discussion about what happens when you break those rules?"

More grumbling with an added hiss or two came from the backseat. "No."

"So now that we're clear on the rules, what exactly is Bobby expecting me to do in exchange for sexual favors with his ex-wife?"

"You know, it's not all quid pro quo. His missus is lonely. It makes him sad to see her like that."

"Right, and?" I pulled into the driveway.

Clarence huffed out a breath. "And he wants you to figure out who did him in and work your death magic on them so that his missus—his ex-missus—is safe."

Good grief. "I don't have any death magic."

"Shh! We're almost home. He'll hear you."

Not my problem. "He should hear me. You've been telling lies. If I remember correctly, Bobby's not a big fan of false-hoods." That *liar, liar pants on fire* chant of his had driven me bonkers since he'd shown up.

"It was more of a fib, a *tiny* white lie." His voice turned whiny. "I was lonely. Bobby talks to me. And he watches TV with me. We're even working on his corporeal form so he can rub my belly."

"*What?*" I lowered my voice to a more reasonable decibel,

and repeated, "What?" A kitty glare waited for me when I looked over my shoulder.

"*You* never rub my belly."

There were simply no words. I was not rubbing any cat's belly. Not a twenty-five-pound bobcat that could slice and dice my wrists, and especially not pornography-watching Clarence, who I was half convinced had been an aging letch before his death.

No.

5

Monday morning

"Just a little rub. That's all I want. Come on," Clarence pleaded.

Now that his secrets were out, both his predilection for British baking shows and the tummy rubs, he wouldn't leave me alone.

At least he'd waited until after I cleaned up the backseat of the car before he started to nag. When I'd parked, he disappeared inside the house, leaving me alone in the garage with nothing but noxious odors for company.

But then he started in and hadn't shut up until I'd locked him out of my bedroom last night. I was considering installing a key lock on my bedroom, because he could manage some surprising tasks with those oversized paws and lack of an opposable digit. It wasn't out of the realm of possibility that he could learn to pick the thumb lock.

First thing in the morning, he was at it again. *Pet me. Scratch my chin. Rub my belly.* He resembled a needy retriever more than any cat I'd met.

I had a few options. Ignore him, in which case I suspected he'd get louder. Placate him—belly rubs and paw massages? Unthinkable. Or distract him.

Bingo. But distract him with what? The only options that came to mind included messy human problems and all the complications they entailed. While I contemplated the problem, Clarence's nagging continued.

"I promise not to bite you. I won't even scratch—much. Come on." He meandered back and forth in front of me as I walked to the fridge.

He'd almost tripped me three times now. I desperately needed to drink my coffee in peace, or I might overcome my distaste for violence and do him serious harm.

"Milk, Clarence. I need milk for my coffee." I waited for him to step away from the fridge door.

He looked at me quizzically. "You don't usually drink your coffee light."

"It's a milk sort of a day. Move along." I nudged him with my foot so I could open the door.

Once I'd dosed my coffee with a solid dollop of milk, I took a drink and tried to think like a rational human being instead of a deranged lunatic.

No joy.

Either Operation Distract began now, or I was going to dropkick the perverted, needy furball across the living room. Enmeshing myself in the messiness of humanity was looking less distressing with each passing minute.

"How 'bout a scratch under the chin? Do a kitty right. Come on."

Drop. Kick.

I sighed. I'd never forgive myself if I booted him, no matter how much Clarence deserved a hard kick to his nether regions.

"So who were these disreputable characters that Bobby

had business dealings with? Because it seems as if he believes they're the ones who offed him."

Clarence stopped crisscrossing in front of me and pinned me with one of his sharp feline gazes. "You wanna help her, don't you? She's one hot babe, especially in that tight, little pink number. The way it hugs her t—"

"Stop."

"I was just gonna say ta-tas. That's not even a dirty word. Or directly to do with your sex life."

One hard look and he grumbled out an apology.

"Who are these bad men that Bobby worked for? Maybe we should start there. If we can quietly solve Bobby's murder and then give the cops a solid tip, Sylvie should be safe. Problem solved." And Clarence couldn't use me having sex with Sylvie as some twisted carrot to keep Bobby hanging around our house.

"He can't remember. Death fugue."

"That's not how it works, Clarence, and you know it. A fugue doesn't impact life memories. That's why it's called death fugue." I sighed. There was another possibility. "He might have Swiss-cheese memory if he went wrong while becoming a ghost."

Clarence shrugged, which in his cat form looked like he was ducking his head.

Which meant that I needed to talk to the ghost himself. Wonderful.

I took a breath, steeling myself for the step I was about to take. The step that dropped me off a very steep cliff. "Bobby! Hello, Bobby. It's Geoff. It's time you and I spoke."

"Uh, boss, he told me before that he couldn't remember who he was working for, just that they were bad guys," Clarence said. "So, maybe they killed him, maybe they didn't, he can't remember. But he does know they were dangerous people."

The "boss" comment threw me for a loop. So much so that when Bobby arrived, he startled me.

Geoff. Geoff's gonna sleep with my wife?

The barely visible, faded, and flickering image of a man in his early to mid-forties appeared in the corner of my living room. But he wasn't looking at me. He was addressing the question to a space near my left kneecap.

Following Bobby's gaze, I found Clarence shaking his head. He caught me watching him and stopped, his eyes wide and innocent. He slowly squeezed them shut and then opened them in what I'd come to recognize as a purely feline expression of satisfaction.

Of course he was happy. He thought he'd made progress in his plan to pimp me out. He was completely incorrigible and also confused. Even if there was anything in my life of that nature to share, I most certainly wouldn't share it with Clarence. There would be no vicarious living through me.

"No, Bobby," I told the faded image in the corner. "I'm not going to sleep with your wife." The ghost's image flickered at a more rapid rate, a sure sign of some extreme emotion, so I added, "But she's beautiful, your ex. Sylvie's a lovely woman. Exceptionally so." The flickering continued, so I muddled along. "I mean, I'd love to have sex with your ex, it's just . . . it's not necessary."

A delicately cleared throat was the first sign that I wasn't alone in my living room. I pivoted toward the sound.

"Your front door was wide open, and when I tapped on the storm door, you didn't respond. I brought a house-warming gift." Sylvie lifted a plate of cookies and watched me with intent interest. "Ah, are you talking to my ex-husband's ghost?"

6

R ed peppers and scalding water never made my face burn so bright.

The poor woman, her ex-husband dead no more than a few weeks, and she walked in on me not only appearing to talk to him, but also declaring my intention of not having sex with her. It was mortifying—for both of us.

Two public declarations regarding my sexual intentions in one day. In my world, that was two too many. Contrary to the evidence, I wasn't sex-obsessed. I spent too much time with a talking bobcat who had the hormonal urges of a teenager, but *he* was the sex-obsessed one.

And since when could a cat, regardless of how clever, work a childproofed door? I was going to have a nice chat with that saleslady about how childproofed my front door was. I distinctly remembered shutting it firmly and the latch catching.

When I emerged from my haze of horrific embarrassment, I found her grinning. "Bobby did tend to have that effect on people."

"What effect?" And what a stupid question. *Get it together, man.*

"Excited, inappropriate utterances." Her brown eyes twinkled back at me, demonstrating an amusement I was sure I wouldn't share in her place.

I blinked dumbly back at her.

"You were saying, before I broke into your house . . . something about it not being necessary for you to have sex with me?" That fetching little dimple that I'd noticed before peeked out and then disappeared.

A throbbing behind my left eye distracted me briefly. "Ah, yes, apologies for—"

Her chuckle interrupted me, and like that, the pain was gone. She waved a hand dismissively. "I blame Bobby."

"No, please accept my apology." But before I could complete a coherent expression of regret, I realized it might be best to address the other topic, the not-sex-related one. "You asked if I was talking to Bobby, your ex-husband. The one who's dead."

She nodded solemnly. "I did. Something to do with you staring at a blank space on the wall and calling it Bobby, then talking about his ex-wife, who I assume to be . . . me. Cookie?"

She pulled back the cellophane covering the pile of cookies. And that was when I got my second whiff of cookies that day.

"You like to bake?" I limited myself to one, thought better of it, and then took two more. The first bite was answer enough to my question. Cookies had the appearance of simplicity, but it was a lie. Creating the *perfect* cookie was an art, and Ms. Baker had mastered the perfect cookie.

"I do." Again the dimple peeked out. "These are all for you."

"Ah." But that was all I could manage with a mouth full of

cookie, so I nodded with what I hoped was sufficient enthusiasm to express my gratitude.

Her eyes crinkled attractively at the corners as she tucked the cellophane back around the cookies. "I'll just set these over here." She pointed at the kitchen table.

Still savoring the large bite I'd taken, I nodded again. Ms. Baker found me amusing, and I wasn't certain how I felt about that.

A plaintive meow chased away my uncertainty. About that particular creature, I had no reservations. "Ignore him. He likes to complain." I shot Clarence a warning look, which he completely ignored, emitting another meow. "About your ex, or, rather, your ex's ghost . . . What are your feelings about ghosts?"

Disregarding my directive to ignore him, Sylvie leaned down and scratched Clarence under his chin. "Aren't you just the handsomest cat ever. Such a big kitty." A thunderous purr startled a chuckle out of her. "And loud." She scratched under his chin and ran her hand down his back. Finally, she said, "I'm not sure what my feelings about ghosts are, but if you're asking whether I believe they exist, then yes, I do."

"You do."

She stood and brushed her hands together. Little tufts of cat hair fell and drifted to the ground. Her firm, clear gaze met mine. "I do, and it seems you do as well. Sink?"

I gestured to the kitchen sink and considered her words.

Bobby wasn't fully himself. He'd either gone wrong when he'd become a ghost or he'd not been the brightest bulb to begin with. Having twice now met Sylvie Baker, I suspected the former.

Then again, he was her *ex*-husband.

But whatever the origin of his decreased mental capacity, was he confused enough to fantasize a threat that didn't exist?

Was Sylvie truly in some kind of danger? I'd been concentrating on ridding my life of a pest. Since cleansing my house seemed unlikely at this point, I was turning to alternatives to addressing his concerns in hopes that a happy ghost would have no need to pester me and might even move on. Immersed in my own headache-inducing, ghostly troubles, I hadn't considered the implication that my pretty neighbor might truly be in harm's way.

The idea that someone intended her harm, even if the idea came from a half-demented ghost, made me uncomfortable.

"While you try to decide whether I'm gullible, silly, or naive, I'll just go ahead and tell you: my grandmother saw ghosts. Actually, she mostly heard ghosts, but every once in a great while, she could see them." She replaced the tea towel she'd used to dry her hands on the hook next to the kitchen window and turned to look at me. Without any sign of her previous levity, she said, "My grandmother was *not* a silly woman. And that's why I believe in ghosts."

Fair enough. Not that I'd considered her silly or gullible or naive. She possessed the kind of happiness that escaped like bubbles into the air for others to admire and enjoy. But she wasn't the least bit silly.

Before I could think twice, I said, "Bobby's been haunting your home and popping in to see us at regular intervals."

A frown creased her forehead. "I was afraid of that."

"You were?" That didn't seem like something that would occur to most people after their ex passed away. Not even a top-twenty concern, if I had to guess.

"If ever a man was going to haunt a woman from beyond the grave, Bobby was a good candidate. He tended toward obsession." Again the wrinkle in her forehead appeared. "Not that he was possessive, nothing like that. He was generally a good man—one who made terrible decisions—but a good man."

"Not always." When she looked at me with a question in her eyes, I tried to clarify, "He didn't always make terrible decisions, because…" The words "you're amazing" didn't exactly trip off my tongue, but I think she got the picture.

The wrinkle disappeared, replaced by the crinkle at the corners of her eyes. "Aren't you sweet, Geoff."

My neck warmed.

A hacking hairball cough reminded me we had an observer. That I could forget Clarence, even for a moment, meant that Sylvie Baker had me tied up in knots.

But there was business to be handled, a threat to be assessed. "Sylvie, about your husband—"

"Ex-husband."

I scanned the room for some sign of Bobby, but he must have run out of juice while we'd been speaking. He'd be recharging now and would be back later to drive me out of my mind.

"Right, your ex-husband. He seems to think that you might be in danger." I shrugged and gave her a sympathetic look. It sounded more than a little crazy voiced aloud. Not that I wasn't worried, but I felt silly saying it.

Even if Bobby had been in some trouble before his death, they weren't married anymore. And she was a hairdresser. Who could possibly want to hurt her? And yet, the thought had me twitching with unease. One moment, my rational mind was convincing me this was ridiculous and the next my gut was telling me it wasn't. This was what happened to my orderly life when the chaos of humanity was invited into it.

Shaking her head, she said, "I can't imagine—"

An eardrum-thumping clap trailed by an ominous vibrating rumble had us both ducking in surprise.

"What in the world?" Sylvie's gaze darted around the room looking for the origin, but she wouldn't find it here.

I knew that sound. Something nearby had exploded.

It looked like my gut might be more clever than my head. I'd bet those fantastic cookies on my kitchen table that the target of the explosion was the house kitty-corner to my own.

7

The good news: it wasn't the house kitty-corner to mine. The bad news: it was the shed in the backyard of the house kitty-corner to mine.

Sylvie was understandably upset. Her shed had been blown to pieces about the same time that I'd been suggesting there just *might* be a *small* possibility that someone wished her harm . . . according to her dead ex-husband.

But beyond "upset," I hadn't a clue how she was handling the explosion or the news of her haunting. She'd emerged from my home to the sight of smoke in her backyard and several helpful neighbors already on the phone with 911. The crowd included a few neighbors I'd met: Mrs. Gonzalez, Mr. and Mrs. Patterson, and Vela George. But there were quite a few new-to-me faces: a tall black man with dark shades who took one look at me and spun on his heel to leave, a group of teenage kids who looked intermittently shocked and fascinated, and a young man who spoke to Mrs. Gonzalez before leaving, possibly her nephew.

Mrs. Gonzalez had embraced Sylvie as she stood in the

middle of the street and watched the rising smoke. With one suspicious glance in my direction, Mrs. Gonzalez hustled Sylvie away from me. They quickly disappeared into Mrs. Gonzalez's home, four houses down from my own. From what little I knew of Mrs. G, Sylvie was either being plied with sweet tea or she was drowning her loss in tequila.

I stayed long enough to watch the authorities arrive, both firemen and police, then retreated indoors.

Clarence followed on my heels, watching as I poured whiskey into a coffee mug and started a pot of coffee. In my experience, Irish coffee was the only reasonable way to drink booze before noon.

"No way you could have known her house was going to get exploded," Clarence said while I waited for the coffee to brew.

His words bordered on considerate, sympathetic even. I eyed him with suspicion.

"What? A cat can't have a little empathy? I mean, I know you want some of that—who wouldn't?—and now it's gonna be hard, what with her crying over her house. Although you could comfort her—"

"Stop while you're still ahead."

"Right." He flicked the back of his ear with his hind foot. "So how about we go for gold here, and I also mention that I'm sorry for leaving the front door open. I was bird-watching earlier and then got distracted."

"The childproofing is on there for a reason." Clarence, out in the world, wreaking whatever havoc popped into his feline brain, was not a scenario I liked to dwell on. But he hadn't left the house, just created another bird-squirrel-neighbor viewing spot, so I relented. "It wasn't your fault I got caught spouting—what did Sylvie say?"

Clarence chuckled. "Excited, inappropriate utterances.

She's cute. And just about your speed, except, you know, with really nice ta-t—"

My throat-clearing efforts produced the desired effect, and Clarence firmly sealed his lips. For about three seconds.

"I'm just saying, I think you're a nice"—he spat, like something nasty had crawled into his mouth—"couple. There. I said it. That's my requisite nice for the day."

"Appreciated. Now, any thoughts about this explosion?"

"Ha!" If Clarence still had a knee, he'd be slapping it. As it was, he bounced in a very un-catlike way. "I knew you couldn't ignore a damsel in distress." He pogoed a few more times. "We're gonna do right by Bobby *and* his old lady. That's my upstanding, do-gooder boss man."

Apparently, Clarence truly had been lonely if he'd developed such an affinity for our ghostly visitor in such a short time. I felt a twinge of guilt for the limited contact he had with the outside world, but he wasn't trustworthy and he was my responsibility.

In a moment of weakness, I reached down and patted him. "We're going to do our best to sort this mess out, I promise."

Clarence purred, and I snatched my hand away.

He blinked his big green eyes at me. "Is this one of those 'never to be spoken of' moments, boss?"

Not answering seemed the best method to discourage him, so I changed the subject. "I'll get you a good scratching post, and you can rub your chin to your heart's content."

Clarence had only called me "boss" when we'd discussed Bobby's situation. Maybe it was an indication of just how important it was to Clarence to help his new friend. Yet another reason to involve myself. Not only was it the right thing to do, but my feline ward was showing some signs of emotional growth. I wanted to encourage any improvement .

. . and it was also likely he would make my life miserable if I didn't take the case. So it looked like I was diving in, even if it would drop me into the deep end of humanity much sooner than I'd anticipated.

"Or you could invite that tight piece of—"

I cleared my throat. So much for Clarence's big heart and good intentions. "Don't start."

He ignored my warning. "As I was saying, you could invite the lovely Sylvie over, and she can scratch that itch for me."

"Clarence, get your mind out of the gutter. Besides, I'm not sure Sylvie will have much time for us, what with our recent disclosure and her shed blowing up. Most people don't look favorably on the supernatural or those who believe in it."

"I don't know. She seemed pretty open-minded to me. You heard what she said about her grandmother."

"We surprised her. We'll see how she feels after she's had a moment to consider it."

Clarence grinned, showing a little fang. "You know, it's always possible that there's no bad guy here. Maybe she was cooking meth in her shed."

His gleeful tone made me roll my eyes. "Really? You think so?" I sat down at the kitchen table after pulling a chair out for him.

Clarence hopped up and eyed me intently before sitting. "I guess not. Your neighborhood doesn't have a *Breaking Bad* flavor. It's more *Leave It to Beaver* meets *The Brady Bunch*."

"With you living here? Try *I Love Lucy*." I rolled my shoulders, working out the kinks. Getting used to a physical body again was proving eventful. "Enough with the sitcoms. We need some intel, and since neither of us has an inside man with the fire department or the police, we need some more local sources." I leveled him with a stare. "Sylvie's off the table for now."

"Sure, sure," he agreed—much too readily. "What are you thinking, boss?"

"I'm thinking the recently dead. Maybe there was a witness." I tilted my head. "Anyone besides Bobby still hanging around?"

Clarence would know, since ghosts appeared to him whether they actively wanted to be seen or not.

"Word of your disinterest in engaging with the spirit world has gotten 'round." Clarence flattened his ears and poked out his nose. "And by word, I mean not nice words."

"Who, me?" I asked. My former rep had been as a polite, escort-your-soul-with-kindness sort of death. But I was *retired*. Couldn't a man get some peace in his golden years?

"You've developed a post-retirement reputation." Clarence sniffed.

I pointed a finger at him. "Don't sneeze on the table."

His ears flattened again. "I wasn't going to. I'm *trying* to be nice, but since you're being such a cat hater, I'll just say it. You've got the rep of an ornery, mean old fart. There, I said it. A cat-hating, unhelpful meanie."

The unhelpful part certainly hit home, primarily because I wanted all of those pesky ghosts to *leave me alone*. If my life was a lawn, I was that guy hollering for the kids to get off it.

Leaning back in my chair, I crossed my arms. "Not the reputation I had as a soul collector, but I'll take it now."

Clarence waggled his kitty eyebrows. It was unsettling to see, even more so than a talking cat whose mouth never moved. "You sure you were so beloved before?"

"Yes, actually. Okay, Clarence. I'll try to be more helpful. Not because I want to clean up my reputation, but because solving Bobby's murder is the right thing to do."

"What about the cat-hating bit? You gonna fix that? Give a clever kitty some extra fish for dinner, maybe?"

His request got exactly the attention it deserved. "So, again, any souls in the area? Besides Bobby. Preferably one who's more intact than Bobby."

Clarence looked as shifty as a cat could look. His gaze darted to the corner of the kitchen ceiling. With a sigh, I couldn't help imagining how bad a poker player he must have been in his human days.

"Are you developing other friendships? Or perhaps hiding some especially persistent spirits? Spirits, like Bobby, to whom you've made certain promises."

He whistled. A whistling bobcat in my kitchen, and he didn't think I'd find that suspicious. "Spill it. And no negotiating." When he hesitated, I reminded him that he'd requested my involvement. "Time to do your bit for this investigation."

Apparently, the moral dilemma hadn't occurred to him, because he looked baffled.

"It's called a conflict of interest, Clarence. Look it up."

"What am I? An attorney?" A little grousing and grumbling and he finally said, "Ginny. She might have been hanging around and seen something. She's grounded at the end of the street."

"Uh-huh. And where exactly did you meet Ginny?"

"Hmmm." His whiskers twitched, and he tripped my finely tuned trouble alarm. Or rather he increased the trouble quotient. With Clarence there was always a baseline of mischief.

Resigned, I asked, "In the house?"

His whiskers practically vibrated, and then his confession came out in a rush: "Yes, in the house. And yes, she might have had a look. And yes, she finds you quite attractive. And yes, she'll be coming by again around nine."

"Nine?" Nine was when I had my nightly soak. My neck heated up. "You invited a peeping . . . ah . . ."

"Tomasina?" Clarence supplied in the most helpful of tones.

"You're getting two days of dry kibble for this. I am not a peep show for your little ghost girlfriends." I shouldn't be surprised. He was an opportunist, and he'd simply found a way to cash in on a beneficial situation. One that involved me bare and in my tub . . . but I still shouldn't be surprised.

Why a ghost would want to catch me in the buff was a more pertinent question. And what exactly was Clarence getting out of it by keeping his trap shut?

A nasty thought occurred. "Is she here now?"

"No." Clarence took one look at my face and said with as earnest a face as a bearded cat could muster, "I swear, she's not."

Because my ghost-possessed bobcat ward was the only one of the two of us who could see, hear, smell, and touch ghosts regardless of whether they wanted to be seen, I had to rely on him. That made my eye twitch more than Bobby's intermittent visitations.

"How do we get in touch with Ginny?"

"Well"—his whiskers twitched—"you usually take a bath around nine, so . . ."

An uncomfortable feeling inched up my spine. "Clarence, you've managed to taint one of life's greatest pleasures and make it feel dirty."

"Life's greatest pleasures *are* dirty, boss. You just haven't figured that out yet."

I refrained from arguing, because what was the point? Clarence might be inhabiting a cat's body, but he was a human letch under all the fur.

"Right. Looks like I have an appointment at nine."

Clarence cleared his throat. "Eight fifty-five. She's particularly fond of the disrobing part."

"Clarence!"

But he was gone before I could snatch anything but a small tuft of hair from his bobtailed butt.

8

Monday afternoon

With several hours to kill and the itch to find the bombing culprit seeping deeper into my skin, I decided to check in on Sylvie.

Not that I was concerned, because I barely knew the woman.

And if she'd been the target, the bomber would have placed the device in her home.

And if she was still upset, she had friends to look after her. She was probably still wrapped in Mrs. Gonzalez's motherly embrace.

As I changed my undershirt and tossed on a clean button-down, I considered my first and then second impressions of Sylvie Baker and modified that last assumption. She was likely back home scheduling contractors to repair her shed and not upset at all.

Either way, my appointment with Ginny the peeping ghost was hours away. I didn't have anything more pressing to fill my time. And if Sylvie called me a lunatic for claiming to talk to dead people and slammed the door in my face, well, at least I'd know she wasn't bawling in her bedroom and that she hadn't been snatched by an evil bomber.

Not that I truly was worried about either of those possibilities.

"I thought we weren't going to bother her," Clarence said as I finished buttoning my shirt.

"*You're* not. And get off my bed." I started to tuck in my shirt.

"Leave it untucked. That kind looks better untucked."

I glanced in the mirror. "Really?"

"Trust me. And roll the sleeves, like a guy who lives in Texas in this decade."

Shirt untucked, sleeves rolled up, but sans Clarence, I headed out the door three minutes later—after debating a shave and deciding against (on Clarence's advice) and brushing my teeth (to the sound of Clarence's catcalls).

It turned out that Sylvie was neither wrapped in Mrs. Gonzalez's ample arms nor contacting contractors. When she answered her door, she had a glass of wine in hand and a board game tucked under her arm. "I was going to call you. Well, I was going to call Cindy—you know Cindy Eckhardt from down the street?—but she has her daughter by herself this evening, and then I remembered how nice you were."

"I was?"

She nodded. "So then I was going to call you."

"Ah. You don't have my number, and it's not listed."

She tipped her wine glass at me. "And then I realized I didn't have your number." Red wine sloshed precariously near the rim of her glass as she toasted me. After taking a sip, she stood very still. "I'm glad you're here now."

"Sylvie?" I watched her list to one side—subtly, but still . . . "Are you tipsy?"

She slugged the last of the wine and beckoned me inside.

"I certainly hope so. I've had three glasses of surprisingly good boxed wine."

I trailed behind her as she led the way to the kitchen. And indeed, a box of red wine waited on the kitchen table, along with a second glass.

After setting the board game on the table, she refilled her glass. She tapped the game, her finger landing on the "O" in Ouija. "Target. If you're ever in a pinch and need help reaching the great beyond, Target is the spot. Wonderful place."

"I'm hoping you managed that trip before all three of those glasses of wine."

Her forehead crinkled. "Of course. Where do you think I got the box of wine?" She turned back to the table and pointed at the glass there with a startled look on her face. "Right. So rude of me. Would you like a glass?"

I shook my head. "You're expecting someone?"

"I told you: I was expecting you, until I didn't call you. But then I was going to fetch you. Maybe after another glass. Wine makes me brave." Her cheeks turned a pretty shade of pink. Then she tapped the board game again and leveled me with an intent look. "You're going to find that sorry son of a gun ex of mine."

Sorry. Really, really sorry. So sorry.

That wouldn't be difficult, because Bobby was back, recharged and hollering in my ear.

All options considered, there really was only one answer. Maybe I was opening up Pandora's box, maybe complicating my life, but Sylvie looked so lost. "He's here, and he's sorry."

Really, really sorry.

Eyes closed, I repeated, "Really, really sorry."

"Where?" She spun around in a circle, miraculously spilling only a few drops of bright red liquid on her kitchen floor. "If this is your fault, Bobby, I will not forgive you. They blew up my shed. My shed, Bobby. My shed is really close to my h-h-home." She swallowed. "The firemen were here for two hours."

Was she about to cry?

I touched her shoulder, which startled her enough to slosh wine down the front of my shirt. And I'd put on a new shirt just for the occasion. Lesson learned: threadbare T-shirts were not only considered stylish, but were also practical, especially for drunk Sylvie visits.

How I'd predict the drunk part, I wasn't sure. Maybe it was just best to invest in a few more decent shirts.

Sylvie tugged on my shirt tails, pulling me closer.

"Wha—"

Then she did it a second time.

I clamped my mouth shut and stood six inches from her, not daring to move a muscle. Then she started to unbutton my shirt. From the bottom. "Whoa."

She stopped, the backs of her hands practically brushing my fly. "What? Don't tell me you're shy. It'll stain if we don't rinse it right away."

Bobby cackled with glee in the background. A shame. I'd forgotten he was here.

I grasped her hands, squeezed them, then let go. "Thank you. I've got it."

"Okay." She shrugged, but—was that disappointment on her face, or just wishful thinking?

Not that I needed that kind of entanglement. I'd only been retired a few weeks and had barely acclimated to being human again. Given this situation and how uncomfortable it made me, I probably *hadn't* fully acclimated. I slid a few buttons free and yanked the shirt over my head.

When I handed it to her, she was frowning at me. Or, rather, my chest.

"What?" I looked down at my undershirt. "It's fine. I'll chuck it in the wash when I get home."

"Hm. My dad used to wear T-shirts like that under his work shirts."

I kept trying to get past World War II-era fashion, but it looked like I was still failing. "Excellent. And how old is he?"

"Oh, no, that's not what I meant." She shook her head. "Not at all. Bobby never wore them, but— Ohmygosh, Bobby! Is he still here?" She pressed the back of her hand to her cheek. "Maybe I've had a bit too much wine."

I pulled out a chair for her, and she sank down into it with a sigh.

I took a few steps to my right and looked out her kitchen window to the backyard. "Understandable." The damp, charred remains of her shed cast a pall over the cheery, flower-filled yard surrounding it. "I'll just . . ." I lifted my shirt, and she nodded then gestured to the kitchen sink.

After giving the wine stain a rinse, I left the shirt to drip in the sink and poured myself a half glass of wine. After I joined Sylvie at the kitchen table, I asked, "What did the firemen tell you?"

She'd crossed her arms on the table, making a pillow for her cheek. She didn't lift her head when she replied, "They said it was a very small explosion. They didn't even suspect anything unusual until I told them what was stored out there."

"I'm sorry, what significance does the contents of the shed have?"

"No gas, no paint. The shed's not even wired for electricity. I used a flashlight when I occasionally went out there."

"I see. No source for a spark and no accelerant. What is stored there? Sorry, *was* stored there?"

"Old paperwork, some clothes, a few pieces of furniture I

couldn't use but didn't want to get rid of. My gran's." Her face looked pinched when she mentioned her grandmother, and that made me feel panicky. Like I should make it all better for her.

As I watched, her lids grew heavier. Before she fell asleep, I asked, "What kind of paperwork?"

"Mmmm." She blinked. "I used to do some bookkeeping before I started cutting hair, when I was still married to Bobby."

My trouble-o-meter dinged—not off the charts, but there was a flutter. "Were all of your records in the shed?"

The soft shush of her breathing was the only answer.

"Sylvie," I called softly. When she didn't respond, I stood up and moved into the living room. "Bobby?" I whispered.

Here!

Clutching my head, I lowered my voice even more. "Whoa, keep it down."

Here.

"Thanks. So, Bobby, do you know who's responsible for destroying the shed?"

Bad people.

Right. Dealing with ghosts who'd left a good part of their cognitive function with their physical bodies wasn't something I'd missed since retiring. Just my luck, Bobby fell in that category. It could be worse. At least he was verbal.

Simple and direct was the key. I tried again. "Did you see anyone near the shed before it blew up?"

Noooo.

His ghostly voice faded off to a moan. Too bad if he wasn't a witness. Whatever he might have done in his life, whoever he'd been when he was alive, he had cared for Sylvie. Enough that his ghostly self was compelled to help her, and he'd be willing to share what he saw. Some ghosts weren't so accommodating.

"Were you here, in the house, when the explosion happened?"

Boom!

My left eye started to twitch. I rubbed it and said, "Quiet, remember?"

Shhhhh.

"So you were here when the explosion happened. How long before the explosion did you come back to Sylvie's house?"

A moan was the only response. Which made sense. Even ghosts with sharp mental acuity could have difficulty with time.

"Where were you when the shed exploded?"

House. No Sylvie. Just Bobby.

And not a single moan. Now, if I could just keep that going . . . "Where were you before the shed exploded?"

Away.

Probably recharging. So not a witness, and if I grilled him anymore on the time line, I was likely to stress him out or confuse him. It looked like his past was the next stop.

"You worked with some bad people."

Very bad. Nasty.

"You think those people murdered you?"

Yes?

A little more certainty would be nice. "Why do you think that?"

Bad people.

Ask a stupid question of a death-fugued, swiss-cheese-brained ghost . . . "Okay, and your ex-wife, you think these 'bad people' want to hurt Sylvie?"

A quiet sob followed by silence was all I got. And after repeated attempts to get his attention failed, I gave up. Either he wasn't talking to me anymore, or he'd gone to that mysterious place ghosts went to gather up the energy necessary to manifest on this plane.

I'd learned nothing useful from Bobby, but I had to give Clarence credit. He had a greater talent for communication than I'd credited him with. That he'd managed to get any specific information out of Bobby was just shy of a miracle.

Looked like it was time to do some research on Bobby's past. I hated research. No, not research, just computers.

A soft snuffling noise coming from the kitchen caught my attention. Sylvie wasn't quite snoring, but her breathing was deep and heavy, not unlike a person who'd had a bit too much wine.

If I left her propped on the kitchen table like that, her neck and back would be in terrible shape when she woke.

Except I wasn't entirely sure that *my* back was up to the task of toting women around.

Her breath hitched and then she sighed.

I couldn't leave her there. Looked like I was about to find out how out of shape my newly reacquired body was in.

9

Monday evening

"Hurry it up, Clarence." Watching him tap on the keyboard with his claws was like watching ice melt. Or water boil. Whichever, it was slow, and the over-the-counter painkiller I'd taken for my back wasn't working nearly as well as advertised.

Sylvie had a figure to die for and was soft in all the right places. Not that I'd done anything inappropriate; she'd been asleep, for heaven's sake. But lifting a grown woman of any size was just as difficult as I'd remembered, a fact my back continued to protest.

Another twinge had me asking if this should be taking quite so long.

Clarence paused with his fluffy paws hovering over the keys. "If you'd get me that voice-recognition software like I'd asked, I'd be a lot faster. And do you even know how hard this is?" He retracted and extended his claws. "These paws were not made for typing. It makes my claws ache like you wouldn't believe."

When he didn't immediately return to the task, I mentally tallied his monthly bribes then gritted my teeth. "Voice-recognition software, got it."

And the incredibly slow tapping started again. "Here, look, I've got something. You can quit with the Mr. Cranky Pants routine."

"If I'm cranky, it's because in about fifteen minutes I'm going to be confronting a peeper instead of enjoying the calming soak I desperately need."

Clarence grunted. "Right. Let's not dwell on past mistakes."

"*Your* past mistakes. *I* didn't invite a ghost to a nightly private viewing of my relaxation ritual."

Clarence ignored that. "So, I've got Bobby's work history, criminal convictions, and some financial information, all for the reasonable sum of nineteen ninety-nine."

Modern technology at work. Sometimes I felt as if life had not only passed me by but had left me in the dust to choke. Wait, nineteen ninety-nine? "How did you pay for that?"

"Ahhh, you know that credit card you thought you hid from me? You might have hidden it, but I memorized the number first. Also, taped to the back of the toilet tank? Really? You'll have to do better."

"Of course, you memorized the numbers, because that's normal behavior." I shook my head. I knew at some point in his past Clarence had counted cards, because he'd told me so. I should have realized a handful of digits and a date wouldn't be a problem.

Large green eyes blinked innocently at me.

I pointed at him. "I'll be canceling that one, so don't even try to use it again. And the next one will not be taped to the toilet tank."

"Or stashed in the freezer, taped to the bottom of a drawer, hidden in a book—"

"That can't be normal." He'd covered every spot that immediately came to mind and then some. His creativity exceeded my own with the freezer. "But we don't have a problem, do we? Because you're not going to steal any of my credit card numbers again, are you?"

He whistled a jaunty tune.

"Clarence, how did someone with such a terrible poker face count cards?"

The tune stopped. "Ah, counting them is easy. Not getting caught is the hard part." He tapped a few keys, and my printer started to whir and spit. "Grab that printout, will you?"

I retrieved the stack of papers, astonished by the amount of information that could be bought for the price of a large delivery pizza. "You weren't kidding. There's some good stuff in here. But I don't see anything criminal. It looks like a few speeding tickets."

"That's the tricky part, since we don't have an inside man at the force. As public citizens, we only get access to convictions. No arrests or anything."

"How do you know this stuff?"

Clarence snorted. "I'm not allergic to technology." He glanced at the computer. "It's called the internet. Give it a try, Geoff. You might like it."

Eh, or not. Seemed like a lot of people who weren't really experts talking about a lot of stuff they didn't really know that much about. Also, when I had tried it, I'd spent a total of fifteen minutes poking around before I felt the mother of all migraines looming.

"It's getting close to date time. You better go get ready." Clarence snickered.

"You have a strange understanding of what constitutes a

date. And I'm not taking my clothes off, you old letch. Not till you can guarantee that she's gone."

"Hmmm."

His noncommittal response didn't reassure me, which meant I had to find a way to detect ghosts without the help of my self-interested housemate.

I was placing my faith in Lilac, the green-haired medium. Good thing I had an appointment with her tomorrow. My strategy was to ease into the problem by starting with ghost detecting. Then, once we tackled detection, I'd hit her with my second request: repelling ghosts. A charm, a cleansing ritual, a spell, there had to be some magical recourse for people who didn't want to interact with the dead.

Also, repelling didn't sound nearly so bad as exterminating, so maybe she'd give it a whirl. Lilac might not have thought she had an answer, but if she put her mind to it and tapped her contacts, I hoped she'd be able to help me.

What had she said? Something about visitors from another plane not being pests. Well, I might also attempt to disabuse her of that naïve notion to see if that improved her motivation to help out a poor haunted man.

"Hey, Geoff." Clarence smacked me with a paw, claws sheathed, thankfully, but it felt like getting hit by a billy club. "Anyone home in there? You gotta get a move on, buddy."

Right. My appointment with the peeper. I rubbed my arm.

"And I really think you should consider stripping down to at least your skivvies before saying anything." He shouted at my retreating back, "I think she's more likely to stick around if she has something to ogle."

A few minutes of running water, and the bathroom mirror was steaming up. I'd tried to keep to the same routine, but most of my nightly ritual occurred without actual thought or planning, so I couldn't be certain I'd mimicked it.

Now was probably about when I was taking off my clothes. I didn't know how those guys in the clubs did it with throngs of screaming women watching. Even with only one silent observer, pulling off my T-shirt felt sleazy.

As I shucked my jeans, I tried to convince myself that being almost naked—in nothing but my boxer briefs—wasn't much worse than going to the pool or the lake. But it just wasn't the same.

Time to speak up or I'd lose the opportunity, because it certainly wasn't normal for me to give myself silent pep talks in the bathroom. Except I had no idea how to begin a polite conversation with this woman. A shame Clarence and I hadn't rehearsed the "what to say" part of this plan.

"Ah, Ginny?"

The still, humid air in the bathroom rippled with what felt like a breeze. That had to be her.

"Ginny, I just had a few questions for you." I heard a feminine gasp and quickly said, "It won't take long, I promise, but it's important."

The silence in the small room felt heavy. Then a second stirring of air, and I suspected, though couldn't be certain, that I was alone.

"Wait a second," I called out.

"She's doing a runner," Clarence said from the other side of the door.

My only hope now was that she hadn't immediately left the house. I paused long enough to pull on my jeans before joining Clarence in my bedroom. I knew this was a terrible plan. Why had I listened to that deranged feline?

The deranged feline who was lounging on my pillow while cleaning his nether regions.

The book I was currently reading, the one I'd picked up in

an attempt to moderate my emotions when dealing with Clarence, mentioned the creation of boundaries and clearly communicating those boundaries. I don't believe the author could possibly have imagined someone like Clarence, and I was beginning to doubt her advice. Violence seemed more appealing with each passing day I spent in his proximity.

One look at my face, and he jumped off and trotted down the hall. He called over his shoulder, "This way, Romeo."

I jogged to catch up.

"What did you say to her?" he asked. "She booked it out of there like her wispy butt was on fire."

Trotting after him, I said, "Nothing offensive. Maybe it was just a terrible idea. Maybe *you* should have asked for her help, since *you* know her."

"Here's the thing. She's a little temperamental, and—"

The sound of glass breaking in the kitchen cut Clarence off and had me stopping in my tracks. It looked like our ghostly visitor had stuck around inside the house after all.

"Uh-oh." Clarence's fluffy rear disappeared around the corner to the living room. "You might have pissed her off, boss."

"How? I said maybe a dozen words to her."

Another loud crash preceded Clarence's disembodied response. "Seems that was enough."

When I rounded the corner and got a good look into the kitchen, I couldn't believe it. She was smashing my condiments on the concrete floor. The refrigerator door hung open and a jar of pickles floated in the air.

The crashing of glass followed by the spray of pickle juice had me backing quietly out of the kitchen. "Clarence, is she saying anything?"

Clarence was frozen near the entry to the kitchen and didn't respond.

"Ginny, I'm very sorry for any misunderstanding."

Though I wasn't. She was a crazy woman. But an apology seemed a sensible sentiment to voice.

A small jar of mayo floated into the air, but this time she didn't smash it on the floor.

Clarence's girly squeal at the near miss when it shattered against the wall behind him would have been entertaining under other circumstances, but my kitchen was starting to look like a food fight gone horribly wrong.

"You don't want to hurt Clarence, Ginny."

Don't I?

Finally, a response . . . except my brain was scrambling to find a reasonable reply. A difficult task, since I frequently wanted to clock Clarence myself. "I know he's a pain—"

A jar of jam landed a few inches closer to Clarence. The bright red goo that splattered on his fur looked a little too like blood.

"Ginny, wait just a second. He's a pain, but he has good intentions." Probably. Maybe.

The rat, he snitched. You wanna squeal, little rat? How about this?

A glass pint of my favorite local milk—un-homogenized and only sold at one farmers market in town—smashed into the wall behind Clarence. Man, I liked that milk.

A glass jar of Dijon mustard floated out of the fridge.

"Ah, Clarence, it's probably a good time to retreat, don't you think?"

"Can't." He still hadn't moved a muscle.

He moves, and I'll smash his little rat brains into the wall.

This was going too far. Ginny had serious anger issues in addition to her unsavory peeping predilections. Either she'd been a nut job as a human, or she was going off as a ghost. Becoming a ghost didn't make you angry or violent. Maybe frustrated if you lost some functionality, and that could definitely happen. Case in point, Bobby. But this much anger was either there to begin with, or Ginny wasn't a particularly fresh specimen and she was losing it.

Just what we needed, two violent crazies in the neighborhood.

There was no subtle way to ask, so I dropped the bomb. "How long have you been a ghost, Ginny?"

The French mustard that she'd pulled from the fridge fell to the ground. I flinched then relaxed slightly when the plastic container bounced.

I'm not crazy.

A quick look around my kitchen said otherwise. "Okay, then tell me how long."

A while . . . but I'm still all here. You know, as much as I ever was.

"Yeah?" Definite pre-death anger issues. "That's good news. So what's got you so upset?"

Ginny flickered into a semi-solid state in front of the open fridge. Semi-solid, several steps up from transparent, meant she was a powerful ghost. And if her clothes, makeup, and hair were anything to go by, she was original to the neighborhood, circa late seventies.

Her long, blonde hair fluttered as if moved by a breeze, and she pointed a finger at Clarence. "He promised me."

"Ginny, sweetheart, I didn't have a choice." Clarence was feeling braver. Maybe it was the lack of a hovering projectile. "We needed to talk to you. And I didn't say anything about . . . you know, just where and when to find you."

Ginny glanced nervously at me, her image flickering. Not a good sign when dealing with an unstable ghost, because that usually meant emotions were running high.

Clarence cleared his throat, and I caught the hint. "I have no idea what he's talking about," I said.

The flickering stopped. "Really?"

"Not a clue. I was looking for a witness, and Clarence said

he knew another ghost in the area. I had a few questions, so Clarence told me where to find you."

The fluttering curls settled into a cloud around her oval face. She'd had a gorgeous head of thick, curly hair—back when she was alive. She was actually quite pretty when she wasn't being psychotic.

She turned her full attention to me, waiting.

"Ah, there was an explosion across the street this morning. Bobby, the ghost haunting the house, was away before it happened and didn't see who might have caused it."

She rolled her eyes. "He's not exactly all there. And he has to recharge all the time. I don't think he'll be around for long."

"He might be gone faster if we could put his mind at ease."

"Oh?" That perked her up. "How can I help?"

Wild mood swings in addition to the anger, violence, and voyeurism issues—and she liked to hang out at *my* house. Just great. "Did you see anyone or anything that might lead us to the person responsible for the explosion?"

"I didn't see who set it. I was on the other end of the street."

That was disappointing. "I see. Perhaps you have some information that might help us find the person?"

She twirled a long curl around her finger. "You have a time frame? You know, when it might have been set?"

Clarence had crept closer while she'd been distracted. He was eyeing the mess on the floor with wide eyes, so I nudged him with my toe. "Clarence thinks three days."

He licked his lips, so I nudged him again. Finally, he grunted. "What?"

"Quit eyeing the condiments. You can't eat any of that." My nose couldn't handle the resulting stomach distress that Clarence would be putting his poor bobcat body through.

He let out a disgruntled growl.

"Three days, huh?" At Clarence's nod, she whistled. "Well, boys, it's a neighbor."

Clarence and I shared a look. Austin suburbia housed a bomber? Not likely. And a bomber who had Sylvie's ex in their sights and happened to live in Sylvie's neighborhood. What were the odds?

My skepticism must have leaked through, because Ginny crossed her arms and cocked her hip. At least the flickering had stopped. "Look, it's like this. This is my neighborhood. I keep an eye out, and unlike loony Bobby, I don't have to disappear every five seconds to recharge. I'm grounded in this plane and to this neighborhood. I see who comes and who goes. And except for a few delivery people"—she stabbed the air with her pointing finger—"the only people who've come and gone on this street for the last three days are people who live here."

"That explains it. It must have been a delivery person."

Arms still crossed, Ginny shook her head. "I watch the postman and the regular delivery men. I like to keep up-to-date. You'd be surprised by what some people around here get up to with their mail orders." She shot me a knowing look.

Since she was a voyeur who enjoyed spying on me in my most private moments, I didn't think she had much room to judge. Especially since my deliveries couldn't be more mundane. But I was all about keeping this conversation civil —and my grocery bill from growing any larger—so I bit my tongue.

"You didn't step away for a little while, maybe long enough for a bomb to be planted?" My question brought back the ghostly breeze.

At least still she wasn't flickering or picking up condiment missiles.

"Geoff, she's grounded to this plane and, like she said, to

this neighborhood," Clarence said. "That means she doesn't disappear in the ether to charge up her ghost battery, but it also means she's limited in her ability to travel." His whiskers twitched—with sympathy? "What's your limit, Gin?"

Her curls fluttered against her pale cheek. "Three blocks. My house is gone, replaced by a generic monster house, the kind that brushes up against the property lines." Her expression turned sad. "They bulldozed my garden."

Ouch. And I knew the house she meant. It was at the very end of the street.

"I apologize, Ginny," I said. "I'm sure you're right; I'm just having a hard time envisioning a scenario that involves one neighbor bombing another." Even saying the word "bombing" in combination with neighbor made me uncomfortable.

The breeze stilled, and her hair settled around her face again. "Why? Almost half your neighbors have moved in within the last eighteen months, and then half of those within the last year. And the kind of people that land on this street . . ." She raised her eyebrows.

"Now that, Ginny, is very interesting. Can you give me a list of the most recent people, counting back, say, six months?"

She smiled warmly. "Of course."

Now didn't seem the ideal moment to ask her to please stop ogling me in the buff, so I just expressed my thanks.

Five minutes later, Clarence and I had a list of ten names. Sylvie was absent, because she'd moved in just over six months ago, but Mrs. Gonzalez was included, as were some other familiar names. And I'd thought Mrs. G was a fixture in the neighborhood.

Once Clarence had declared the room Ginny-free, I turned a hand to tidying. I didn't want to give my cleaning lady any reason to think something untoward was happening in the house, even if there was. She cleaned, she washed and ironed, and she even cooked a bit. The woman was a gem, and I wasn't losing her over some ghostly contretemps.

Clarence's eyes were huge as he watched me sweep up glass and goo. This hardly qualified as food and still he was eyeballing it like it was a feast. That really seemed more doglike than cat, but Clarence was a man unto himself.

Before I forgot, I asked him, "What was Ginny so worried that you'd told me?"

"Oh, that." He licked his lips. "She's actually not as much a peeper as a girl in love."

I carefully set down the piece of glass I'd picked up. "I'm sorry, what?"

"Hm, yeah, Ginny's in love." Clarence turned his brilliant green eyes toward me. "Ever since you tried to collect her soul back in the seventies. Guess that didn't work out so great? Since she's here and all."

No. No way. I'd remember her. And a failed collection? I didn't think so. I hadn't made those kinds of mistakes.

"That's not right." Then I remembered. Suicide. A twenty-four-year-old woman found hanging in the living room. It hadn't been my assignment originally, but I'd received it last minute and arrived several minutes after her death.

That I'd forgotten a soul collection so close to my own home was more than surprising. That I'd not recognized her, even considering the changes in her appearance brought about by crossing over, was so unlikely as to be practically impossible.

Except that I had.

"Genevieve, that was her name." I chucked the last of the large glass shards in the trash. "That's all she would say. I couldn't get anything else out of her. I assumed death fugue, but I arrived long enough after death that she'd already begun to leave her body."

"That's a nasty, big black mark for you guys. What were

you doing, catching a catnap when the call went out?" He looked disappointed, as if he had any kind of expectations regarding my proficiency or lack thereof.

"Not that it's any of your business, but it was a last-minute assignment change and couldn't be helped."

"Too bad, since she was probably scared out of her mind."

I stepped away from the gooey mess and turned my full attention to Clarence. "She would have barely had long enough to realize she was dead. Questions about the great beyond and what was to come weren't even a glimmer."

"I know that. I'm talking about the way she died." His attention was drifting back to the food. "Any idea if cats can eat pickles? I'm thinking yes, because they smell *really* good." He licked his lips.

"I don't know." I stepped between him and the glass-pebbled pickles. "Clarence, pay attention. What do you mean about the way she died? She killed herself. Tragic, but—"

"No." His head snaked around my leg but his haunches stayed firmly planted on the ground.

"No what?" When my question failed to grab his attention, I snapped my fingers in front of his face.

He flashed a little fang at me then shook his head. "Sorry. I think I'm overdue a meal. I mean, no, she didn't kill herself. She was murdered. She told me so."

And it hit me, my memories of the scene coming back in a rush. It had been all wrong.

A woman hanging herself should have been my first clue. It happened, but it was hardly common. And something had just felt off—still felt off. Why were my recollections so hesitant to surface?

Back then, I'd been a soul collector. Finding out the how and the who of deaths hadn't been my responsibility. But that was then and this was now. As a *retired* soul collector, my time was my own.

"When Sylvie's safe, you and I are going to have a look at Genevieve's death."

"We are?" Clarence asked, but he had the largest, most Cheshire-like grin plastered to his face that I'd ever seen him wear. "I think that's an excellent idea, boss."

Clarence was on board. No huge surprise, since he complained daily of soul-crushing boredom.

But there was something weighing heavier on me than Genevieve's possible murder and my unnaturally faded recollections. Clarence was wrong about my competence. I *had* collected her soul. Collected it and delivered it.

How in the hell had she come back?

Tuesday morning

"Take me with you. Come on, you know you want to."
Clarence stalked in front of me as I prepared to head out the door.

Much as I tried to concentrate—on Bobby's disreputable history, on solving Sylvie's bombing debacle, and to a lesser degree, on the truly baffling existence of Genevieve on this plane—I couldn't. Not while who knew what ghosts hovered around without my knowledge.

And I certainly hadn't been able to take a bath last night. A five-minute shower this morning was the best I'd managed, and while my back was feeling better, I still would have liked a nice soak. I'd never considered myself particularly self-conscious about my body, but having been the target of a voyeur for days, if not weeks—one with a particular interest in seeing me in the buff—had made me a little more so.

I needed Lilac's help. She was the only person besides Clarence I knew might have a connection to the other side and also might have useful contacts. And she'd been willing to bump my appointment up for a nice little bonus.

Careful not to kick Clarence—much as the fluffy perv deserved it—I walked the remaining five feet to the garage door and grabbed my keys off the peg next to the door. "I looked up that public-access thing."

Did I hear the faint whistling tune of a guilty cat?

"Clarence."

"What? It's a thing, emotional support animals. I figure you used to be death, so you probably have a lot of unresolved issues. Who better to utilize an emotional support cat than the guy who's been death?" He waggled his nonexistent eyebrows at me.

"One of the deaths, and don't do that when other people are around. It looks really bizarre."

"Don't do what?" He plopped down on the stained concrete floor like it was a down bed, then sprawled out with an abandon my knees and back envied. Stretched out like that, he looked twice his size.

"Never mind. My point was that there's no such thing as a public-access cat." I stepped over him, refusing to touch on the topic of my post-soul-collector psychological needs. "A little research revealed some startling facts. For one, claiming that you're an emotional support animal is probably some kind of federal crime."

His voice took on a whiny pitch. "But I wanna go with you. I hate staying at the house all day long. It's bo-ring. So boring. Dullsville." He rolled onto his side, displaying his fluffy underbelly as he clenched and unclenched his claws, kneading the air.

"And the cardinals in the backyard?" I eyed him critically. He knew I knew about those birds.

His whiskers twitched.

I'd seen him staring for half an hour or more the other day. "Hm?"

"Okay, except for Mr. and Mrs. Red, your place is the worst sort of dull. There's not even any porn since you blocked all the good channels. No pay-per-view. No instant-watch rentals of any kind. You suck."

"I pay the bills. And since you have no money . . ." I paused, waiting to see if he denied it. I had my suspicions about Clarence, and one of them was that he had a stash of cash socked away. "Right. Since you have no money, you're stuck with me paying the bills and that includes making the call on which programs we have in the house."

A grumbling/growling combo emerged from Clarence's throat.

Was he becoming more catlike, or was that just my imagination?

"So, take me with, and if Lilac won't let me come in, you can leave me in the car." He gave me his sad cat face.

"Ugh. Just stop that. I told you before: you don't look sad when you do that, just demented."

His features resumed their more natural, smug expression. "So I'm in?"

"You're in." I met his gaze and gave him a hard look. "But if you end up in the car, and someone calls animal control, you're never leaving the house again."

His eyes widened.

"I mean it."

He growled again, but it was distinctly human this time. "Fine. I'll keep a low profile."

Clarence convinced me to take him inside when we arrived, swearing he'd be on his best behavior until we got the okay for him to stay for the session.

So I brought him in with me to ask if he might stay, even

though he wasn't actually my emotional support cat. My second mistake.

The first had been threatening him with house arrest if he got caught in the car and got me in trouble.

To give Clarence credit, he was exceptionally polite when he broke all the rules, opened his yap, and (very sweetly) begged Lilac's understanding. He mentioned hot cars, uncomfortable seat cushions, and his general desire to be entertained and not bored out of his mind in the car. Then he went on to detail his exact level of boredom in my home, including the lack of porn, and explained that he couldn't risk house arrest by staying in the car outside.

He'd have blathered on indefinitely if I hadn't shut him up with a nudge (kick) to his furry posterior. In my defense, he'd ignored my other, less physical attempts to interrupt him.

Once he grunted then shut his trap, Lilac backed up several feet and stared.

For a while.

Eventually, she said, "Are you a ventriloquist or something?"

"Or something," Clarence said with a chuckle, his amusement a clear indication he was oblivious to the repercussions of his actions. Nothing but dry kibble stretched into his future, and any minute now he was going to figure that out.

Regret was only one of the many emotions I experienced as I considered dropkicking Clarence across the room. Regret that I hadn't left the furry idiot in the car, or better yet, at home. Anger that I'd been stupid enough to fall for his best-behavior act.

He'd outed himself, never once considering that it was my rear on the line if anything went awry. Anything like, say, a giant leak of supernatural info into the mundane world. Dry kibble was just the beginning of what I had planned for his meddling, furry hind end.

"Do it again." Lilac's request yanked me out of my torture-leaning musings—and just when I was getting to the good parts.

"Okay," Clarence said in the most agreeable tone I'd ever heard come out of his fanged mouth. "Finally, a discerning ear. You have no idea how hard it's been, being the silent companion to Mr. Straight and Narrow here. This guy, he's a complete dud in the conversation arena. You should have seen him try to make small talk with our neighbor. She is one fine piece of—"

"Tsch. That's enough." She held up her hand, her gaze flitting between Clarence and me.

"I know. It's unsettling." I shot Clarence a nasty look that couldn't come close to expressing how completely screwed he was. "Hearing the words but having no visual cues is unnerving, but trust me, it would be worse if his mouth moved."

"Uh-huh." She seemed to be taking it really well. No fainting, praying, nor exorcising of demons. Not yet. Her gaze zeroed in on Clarence's mouth. "And how exactly is he talking? Since his mouth isn't moving."

"Ah. It's not actually the cat who's talking. Cats don't have the requisite anatomy for speech." She gave me an exasperated, you're-an-idiot look, so I hurried up the explanation. "The cat's possessed by a talking ghost."

Her eyes widened and her nostrils flared—but she didn't say a word.

In a stage whisper that the neighbors could probably hear, Clarence said, "I think she might be having a meltdown."

One warning glance had him whistling away.

Lilac shook her head. "He whistles, too?"

"Yeah. It's incredibly annoying. But yes. If you can think of him as deceased, as a ghost and not a cat, then it's easier."

"A powerful and exceptionally talented ghost." Clarence stretched then collapsed in a heap of fur, looking far too pleased with himself.

She made a strangled sound.

The man's ego knew no bounds, and the cat knew no place he couldn't make himself comfortable. The combination of human and feline traits was normally jarring, but right now it was making my left eye twitch with the hint of a looming migraine.

"I'm usually an open-minded person." Lilac paused as if her next thought had slipped away. I was guessing there was a "but" waiting in the wings.

"And we'll just wait while the green-haired, positive-energy medium lady states the obvious." Clarence snickered until I shot him a warning look.

Lilac shifted to face me more squarely, thereby excluding Clarence from the conversation. "So, let's say, in my open-mindedness, that I might just believe you. What's your deal? Why do you need me if you're hanging out with a possessed cat?" She squinted, examining me like I was a nasty bug she might squish, then took another step back. "Wait, are you possessed, too?"

"Oh, no. He's death."

"Clarence, will you stop it with the death talk?" I said. "It's creepy."

Lilac snatched a crystal off the shelf next to her—not a particularly useful one, in my opinion—and clutched it tightly in her fist. "So . . . you *are* death or you're *not* death?"

"One of the deaths. And no, not anymore."

"One of . . . Wait, what do you mean, 'not anymore'? What does that mean? How can you not be death *anymore*?" She was inching toward the side table where her cell phone was stashed.

She was probably rethinking her decision to meet us

alone again. I sighed. She seemed like such a nice lady. She had good energy.

"I'm retired."

Hysterical laughter gurgled from her throat. "Retired?" she asked, her voice pitched much higher than before.

How was having a retired death in your store worse than having a working death in your store? I really was out of touch. "Retired, as in, I don't do that kind of work anymore. Retired, as in, with a pension and healthcare. My prescription plan could use a little work and my dental isn't the best, but otherwise, it's a pretty nice package."

She broke out in belly-deep laughter. Wiping at the tears in her eyes, she said, "You're kidding." But the look on my face must have said otherwise, because she stilled, tilted her head, and blew out a harsh breath. "You're not kidding."

"Yes! Score one for Team Death." If he'd had a fist to pump, I was sure Clarence would have been pumping away. As it was, he had a creepy Cheshire grin plastered to his face.

"Retired," I reminded him. He really liked to forget that part.

"Team Retired Death?" His grin faded a little. "No, that doesn't work."

Lilac tucked her hair behind her ear. "If you were death—"

"One of the deaths. There's a bunch of us." I shrugged. "It's a big job."

"Okay. That's what you used to be, but you're a normal guy now?"

That was sticky, so while I stuck to the truth, I omitted some information. "I'm human."

"Uh-huh. You're human, but you used to be death."

"I get that it's confusing, surprising, disturbing—but if you're good with Clarence being possessed and me being retired, can we talk about my problem?" I wasn't insensitive

—at least, *I* didn't think so. It was just that sometimes people dealt with stressful situations better if they had a specific task to focus on.

"Out." She said it quietly at first, so I might not have moved as quickly as I ought. "Out. Out, out, out, out! Get out of my shop right now!"

Perhaps I'd miscalculated in requesting her help. I rubbed my ears after she hit a particularly high note. Her response didn't seem in alignment with the new age feel of her shop.

"*Out!*"

Definitely miscalculated.

11

Tuesday late morning

Lilac hadn't been in the proper state of mind for a consult—her shrill demands that we leave might have tipped me off—but I'd managed to leave my card with a scribbled note on the back before making a hasty exit. Waiting around until she'd calmed down hadn't been an option in case she decided to call the police.

Leaving her in that unsettled state had been a gamble. She might talk, she might not, and if she did, there was always the possibility of someone believing her. But I was wagering she'd keep it to herself. That she'd consider the possibilities. Lilac seemed like a lady who was open to the possibilities.

And if she did tattle to the world, there was always the looney bin. Denial was my friend, and I'd deny, deny, deny till the cows came home, in the hopes that she would be the one who'd end up in a room with padded walls and not me.

Each of those scenarios involved risk, which resulted in a corresponding amount of stress. Added to that, I still didn't feel comfortable in my own home. The failure of my appointment with Lilac to produce even the hint of a viable ghost repellant or warning system meant that I hadn't a clue how pest-ridden my place was. Exactly how many ghosts had Clarence not told me about? And were they hovering around in the corners of my home right now?

Which was how I ended up at the library.

I liked libraries.

They were quiet, peaceful places. They also weren't likely to be the scenes of murder or suicide, and highly unlikely to have had any event transpire within their walls that would make a ghost more likely to reside there.

My neighborhood library was set apart from the residential area slightly, so I had hopes that it didn't get short-range ghostly travelers.

Without the threat of a ghostly pest peering invisibly over my shoulder, I could think. And with Clarence absent, I could think without interruption.

Even Clarence yielded when I mentioned my destination. He'd finally caved on the emotional support cat issue, since landing me in federal prison—an unlikely end, but one I nonetheless had played up as a possibility—would result in my replacement. A known evil was better than an unknown in Clarence's eyes, or so it seemed.

It was frustrating that I'd landed amid so many ghosts with the purchase of my new home.

Ghosts weren't actually all that common, since they usually involved a failed soul collection. I'd have said *always* involved a failed collection, but it seemed I'd never understood those rules, or they'd changed at some point, because now there was Ginny.

A young woman saw me waiting at the help desk and waved.

She looked like she was in her twenties, though age was

difficult for me to gauge since my return to the human fold. Jeans, a T-shirt, a beautiful porcelain complexion, and an open, friendly expression made this particular librarian unlike any I'd seen when I'd been human the first time around.

Then I landed on a reasonable explanation. "Are you a volunteer here?"

She grinned. "I'm a librarian."

Ah. Somewhat awkward. I flashed her an apologetic and slightly embarrassed smile. "Sorry about that."

"No problem," she said, her cheerful demeanor intact. "How can I help you?"

"I'm looking for information about a death that occurred in the mid-to-late seventies. I have a first name and an address, but that's it."

"Did you start your research online?" She motioned for me to step to the side of the help desk, where her computer was located.

And I was, once again, revealed to be an archaic outsider.

"I'm not very comfortable with computers." I gave her an embarrassed, apologetic smile. "I came here first."

Her grin reappeared, so I'd either salvaged a little charm from the old days or she was that glad to have the library be a first port of call. Since the parking lot had contained a total of three cars, I suspected the latter.

"If there's information available, I can certainly help you find it." She held out her hand. "I'm Avery."

First names on initial introduction—yet another sign of the changing times. I grasped her hand. "Geoff. It's a pleasure to make your acquaintance."

Avery pulled a pad of paper closer and picked up a pen, her demeanor becoming businesslike. "Let's see what we can find."

After jotting down what little I knew—first name, age at

death, home address, and suspected cause of death—she sat down in front of her computer and pulled up a newspaper clearinghouse. "It contains articles and citations, so with a little luck . . ." Her voice drifted away as her attention was consumed by the screen.

Several minutes later, Avery had a potential name. "Genevieve isn't that common of a first name in the obituaries, so I'm only finding a few in the Austin area, and only one who died at age twenty-four. Genevieve Weber. Cause of death isn't listed, but it wouldn't be in the case of suicide."

"Are there any other details?"

Avery nodded. "Just a second, and I'll print it out for you. If this is the person you're looking for, there's a second citation, but you'll have to go to the Austin History Center to find it. That's the local history division of the library," she added when I gave her a blank look. "The local paper is archived there."

"Ah, I see. Thank you." I had visions of dusty stacks of newspapers, but that probably wasn't how it worked at all. Another adventure for another day.

When she returned with the printout, I discovered the article had a picture—a picture of Ginny. I had a name: Genevieve Weber. Nothing I couldn't get from Ginny herself, considering she didn't suffer from Bobby's Swiss-cheese brain, but she also wasn't as predictably accommodating as Bobby. It was a good start: a name, an obit, and another article that would hopefully shed more light on her death.

Next on my list was a browse of the nonfiction section. I gave up on a computer book about two seconds after I started looking, realizing that perhaps a book wasn't the best avenue to further my education. Better to ask my helpful librarian about that one.

That left the fiction section. I spent a pleasant hour losing myself in the rows and rows of stories. When I was done, I had two books and a much clearer head. I was once again ready to head to my house and face the ghosts, or not face them if they were lurking. Except my eye was drawn to the nonfiction section again—perhaps there was something here that could help my ghost problem.

I briefly considered asking, but Avery had been so helpful that I didn't want to risk a bad impression. Requesting literature on possessions, hauntings, exorcisms, and hoodoo in general probably wouldn't be viewed in the most positive of lights.

I turned away from the rows of books and all their potential to look for the helpful librarian. There might be something else she could help me with. I found her behind the help desk on the phone.

When she hung up, I said, "Perhaps you can recommend some computer classes? For someone who's not quite up-to-date on the technology of today?"

"As long as you don't stop dropping by the library, absolutely." She grinned.

Was she flirting with me? No, every friendly woman wasn't hitting on me, and it was indelicate to even suspect it.

"I don't anticipate that will be a problem." Especially since I'd experienced no ghostly disturbances. Not that they couldn't be lurking—but I was clinging to this space as my haven, and I refused to let reality intrude.

She pulled a sheet out from a drawer and pointed to a list of classes. Most had something like "beginning" or "101" in the title. "Do you think any of these might be helpful?"

With a sigh, I said, "Yes, probably all of them."

"Ah, I see." After sorting through the options with me, she hesitantly recommended a class on how to use computers. "If you're sure this won't be too basic for you?" In a much lower voice, she said, "Our typical customer for this class is quite a bit older than you."

"Oh, I don't know. Looks can be deceiving." The inquisitive tilt of her head had me quickly adding, "But no, I don't think it's too basic. This class is perfect for me. How do I sign up?"

12

Tuesday mid-afternoon

"I can't believe that you gave me homework. What am I, twelve?" Clarence huffed as he flounced his way to the printer, but it was all bluster backed by no real emotion.

"Give me a break. It's not like you had anything else to do." Unless he'd broken his promise to only use my backup credit card for background checks. Now that I'd canceled my other credit card, the card I'd given him was the only one I had.

And Clarence probably knew that. My trouble alarm was ringing, loud and clear.

Wide, innocent feline eyes stared back at me.

"I'm checking my charges tonight. Actually, I'm checking my charges every night until I get a new credit card."

He plopped down in front of my fancy wireless printer. "You're so cheap. Why can't I have a little fun?" He extended and retracted his claws a few times. "My kitty fingers are exhausted and my claws ache. You owe me some porn for my pain and suffering. Just a little. An hour. Watching an hour of porn is almost like not watching porn at all."

"Stop. Every time you start bargaining with me, I feel like I need to scrub the resulting images from my brain. The least you could do is come up with something I might actually agree to."

"An egg for dinner."

That had been too easy. Worried there was a trap I'd missed, I agreed.

"Benedict, with hollandaise sauce."

"I have no idea how to make that."

"Hm." He flexed his claws, kneading the air repeatedly. "My poor claws. I think I'm developing early onset kitty arthritis."

I crossed my arms. "Spit it out. What do you want?"

"I bet Sylvie makes a mean hollandaise sauce." His beard quivered.

"Fine, one eggs Benedict with hollandaise sauce cooked by Sylvie, assuming she cooks eggs Benedict."

His beard quivered a little more. "Two eggs."

"Fine. Two eggs and you leave my credit card alone long enough to let me cancel the thing."

His quivering beard gave way to a full-body chuckle. Which was all kinds of wrong. As Clarence's ghostly human self gave voice to his amusement, his physical bobcat self rolled over on his back and wallowed with his feet waving in the air.

"All right. Enough."

A few more wriggles and Clarence rolled to his feet. "I knew you had a thing for her. It was the cookies, wasn't it?"

"No clue what you mean." The cookies definitely helped.

"You know. The woman smells like vanilla and sugar, like fresh-baked pastries. Like the best cookies ever. That has to appeal to your wholesome soul on some deeper level. And she brought over those sugar cookies, the ones you claimed made your stomach smile." He plopped down on his haunches and started to groom his right front paw. He paused. "They were delicious." Then resumed bathing his foot.

The "mystery" of the vanishing cookies was solved. As was the question of whether bobcats could eat pastries with no deleterious effects.

"Yeah, so what did you dig up on the neighbors?" I rested my hip against the desk. It might take a while to pry all the information out of him.

Clarence's supposed "homework" had been to pull backgrounds on all the neighbors who appeared on Ginny's list.

Clarence gave his paw a last lick then settled back squarely on his haunches. "I'll tell you if you guarantee me immunity for past bad acts, including all credit card transactions, but also any other related illegal activities."

"What have you done?"

"Are you familiar with the term 'hacking'?"

With a sigh, I settled into my desk chair. This just kept getting worse. What did I do to deserve a burden like Clarence? Here was yet another reason to catch myself up on technology. Clarence wasn't the kind of person I wanted to be dependent upon.

"I am familiar with the term, but I didn't know you possessed that particular skill set."

He lifted a paw and flexed his claws. "With these digits? No. Hunting and pecking the few keys here and there is hard enough, and it's not within my current skill set. Not that I couldn't learn if I wanted to. Unlike you, I try to keep current. But it hasn't been a priority, given the thriving supply chain."

Thank goodness for small favors. Wait—thriving supply chain? "What exactly did you do, Clarence?"

"Ah, so, I might have used your credit card to purchase some credits that I bounced around a bit and then eventually used to purchase some highly illegal services, including, but perhaps not limited to, retrieval of credit card and phone records." He gave me his mournful look, the one that made him look demented. "I still get my eggs Benedict, right?"

"Are you planning to use my card again?"

He shook his head with substantial vigor.

"I suppose you're still getting your eggs, then."

"About your credit card . . . It might be best if you don't use it again either."

And there was my eye twitch, back with a vengeance. "I swear, Clarence, I've had a perpetual headache since you came to live with me."

"You sure it's me, boss?" When I glared at him, he said, "Hey, I'm not the only change in your life. The big guys in charge made you human again around the time I was assigned to you. Just consider, maybe that stress you're toting around isn't about me. Maybe it's being human again." He sighed. "I mean, how long's it been since you got laid? You've been a soul collector over half a century. That's a long time to go with no body—and no tail."

My glare must have finally penetrated, because he stopped talking. "If you're done talking about my sex life?"

"Your *lack* of sex life, more like. Yeah, yeah. Falling on deaf ears and all, but it would do you a world of good to . . . Right, never mind. So, I have good news."

"I would hope so, since it's possible your illegal shenanigans will get me put in jail and you in a zoo."

His jaw fell open. "A zoo?"

"You're a wild animal, Clarence. Did you not think that through?" I tapped the desk. "Come on, what have you got?"

If a cat could frown, he was definitely doing it. "From our original list of ten names, I've crossed off several who were traveling. A bit of luck for us that the explosion happened shortly before the school year started up again. It seems everyone with a kid and two pennies to rub together takes a vacation about that time."

"Oh. That is good news." Before I could start to feel more charitably inclined, I reminded myself: hacking by proxy, credit card abuse. No need to hold a grudge, but I also couldn't let him completely skate on his illegal activities. "That leaves how many people still on the list?"

"Oh, I'm not done. I analyzed the background information in combination with the phone records and credit usage to pinpoint Sylvie's whereabouts over the three days prior to the blast."

"Sylvie? Ah, I see. You're thinking a bomber wouldn't have placed the device while she was home. I wouldn't exclude the possibility, but you're likely right."

He gave me a lopsided grin that showcased one fang. "Thanks, boss. There's more. I looked at the neighbor's dog's schedule, and—"

"Wait, what?"

"Sylvie's neighbors, the ones to her left when you face the house, they have a dog who barks at everything. That's the same side of the house—"

"As the shed. Clever, Clarence."

Was that a purr?

Clarence cleared his throat. "So the dog is inside all night long and during work hours, but outside when either one of them is home. The couple who live there have different schedules."

"And this dog's schedule is that predictable? When they're home, he's definitely outside."

"I don't think they like him. I mean, who does that? He's allowed in the house, but only when they aren't there. It's really weird. But my newly acquired four-legged perspective might be clouding my judgment."

"Maybe." I started to do the math on the intertwining work schedules, then factored in sleeping. Wait. "Clarence, how certain are you of this schedule? Because you can't get all of this from credit card and phone records."

He started to whistle.

Did I even want to know? For Sylvie's sake, I guess I had to ask. "How do you know the dog's schedule, Clarence?"

I knew the answer was going to be cringe-worthy. I knew it, and yet when it came . . .

"There's this Persian next door." He coughed. "You know, I'm kind of a cat, when you consider all the factors, and I only see people—"

"Ugh. Clarence, there's lecherous and there's beyond the pale. I'm not sure I can evict those particular images from my memory. Thank you so very much."

"Geoff, look, it's like this: a guy gets confused when part of his parts are cat and part of his parts are man, but I'm not talking about getting action. That would be weird. Even I know that." He paused, then added in a serious voice, "Cats are fun to watch, and not for the reasons you're thinking. Being in this body has an effect on me. I don't always know whether I'm being entirely myself or being influenced by subtle feline tendencies. String has never been so fascinating." He shook his head. "Look, watching helps me figure out what's what—what's me, what's cat, what's cat-influenced me."

He looked deadly serious. The speech he'd just given was probably the most serious I'd ever heard from him.

"Oh." Guilt tapped me on the shoulder. Maybe best not to leap to conclusions when dealing with this and last century's most anomalous ghostly possession. "So, you've been conducting something like an anthropological study?"

Clarence made an exasperated sound. "That makes me sound like you, but sure, like anthropology. If we're talking hotties and sex, I'm all about humans—but I don't have the requisite equipment. If we're talking cats, I like to watch how they interact with people and each other, what their mannerisms are—but I have zero attraction for the four-legged furries."

"I understand, and I apologize."

"If you're really sorry, you'll give me some of the juicy details when you and Sylvie start getting busy."

And he was back to being the disgusting perv I knew and didn't quite love. "That will never happen. Was any part of you ever a gentleman, Clarence? Never mind, just give me the short list."

Clarence grumbled, but he did. And it was short: three households were left. Granted, there was a backup list of people who were much less likely to have stashed the device for various reasons but couldn't be completely ruled out. But three families—four people, assuming a toddler wasn't capable—were a reasonable suspect list.

I ran my finger down the list. "I've got Mrs. Gonzalez and her nephew Nicky. Then, in the Eckhardt household, I've got Mrs. Cynthia Eckhardt, but we're excluding the husband and the toddler. And then there's Tamara Gilroy, the sole occupant in her house."

"That one's suspicious."

"Oh, you know her?" A quick glance at the address showed her living right down the road, maybe six to eight houses away, on the same side of the street as Sylvie. "I don't recall ever seeing her."

"Exactly! And she lives alone. All by herself in that house."

Not really odd, so far as I could tell, so I just shook my head.

Clarence leveled me with a green-eyed stare. "That's weird, I'm telling you. Oh, and she has red hair."

"Because red hair is relevant. Clarence, do you have any actual evidence—other than an inability to rule her out and some bizarre and very outdated notions about women—that points to her guilt?"

"Outdated? Everyone knows red-headed women are fiery!"

His indignation was misplaced and outright bizarre. He had some old attitudes. He was, I suspected, older than me—though my bosses hadn't told me anything about his human life when he'd been assigned to me.

But regardless of his age, Clarence had managed to stay abreast of cultural changes much better than I had. His adeptness with a computer, for one. The "red-headed woman living alone" business was a throwback to an earlier era and unworthy of him—even being the lecherous geezer that he was.

"We're going to say that Tamara is equally as suspect as the other people on the list and leave it at that." I ignored his sulky look.

"Can we put her on the top of the list? Just interview her first?"

And that was something to look forward to: interviews. It had to happen, but I didn't have to like it. It sounded like me inserting myself even more into the neighborhood, the community, the world of people in general.

My plans of slow integration burst into flames. Actually, they'd already burst. Now I was just poking at the embers and sulking, which was juvenile. Interviews, right. When viewed through another lens, this was an opportunity to meet my neighbors.

"Yes, we can visit her first," I said with a forced cheerfulness. I read somewhere that "faking it until you make it" was a strategy that might have merit.

It looked like some of our neighbors were getting a visit from me and my friendly cat. A reverse welcome to the neighborhood, if there was such a thing.

Fake cheeriness aside, it still sounded painful.

Tuesday mid-afternoon

T amara Gilroy was a witch.
Not the "check out a book and learn spells" kind.
And not the religious practitioner variety. Tamara was the
hereditary type. And with witches, it was all about lineage,
family, and connections—so what was Tamara doing here,
on my gentrifying South Austin street?

"Ha, I told you," Clarence stage whispered. "Didn't I tell
you?"

"Just because a person has a few herbs growing around
the house doesn't make them a witch."

In a very un-catlike act, Clarence stood on his back legs
and pointed, claw extended, to a wind chime hung near the
front door.

Pretty glass charms tinkled merrily as they gently jostled
each other. I identified a few protection charms, one for
health and wellness, one for abundant growth—which might
explain, in part, the flourishing herbs we'd seen in her front
yard—but there were also several that were foreign to me.

And while they gently swayed and chimed in a harmless, even soothing way, it was impossible to ignore the fact that there was no breeze.

The door swung open, revealing a pleasant, though perhaps not particularly remarkable, woman. Average height, plump in a pretty, motherly, soft-around-the-edges way, light brown hair that was tucked up in a loose knot, and grass-green eyes. I hastily revised my opinion. Those eyes. She had the most beautiful light green eyes. "Ow."

Clarence carefully extracted his claws from first my leg and then my jeans, where he'd left at least a few puncture marks.

Tamara chuckled. "Smart cat." She leaned down and looked closer. "Hm, not quite a cat." Returning her attention to me, she said, "I hear that you're supposed to be a retired teacher."

I hadn't had dealings with witches, so I only knew what others said. They were apparently wily, always older than they looked, and not completely trustworthy. But I had to consider the source. Soul collectors were their own kind of odd, and tended to be cliquish and leery of outsiders.

"And you're supposed to be a redhead." Clarence started to back slowly away without taking his eyes off her.

"Ah." She smiled broadly. "He speaks. What a clever kitty. And yes, I was a redhead . . . once. Have you been hacking into my past, kitty?"

Her smile was inviting, but her words sounded vaguely threatening. And her casual use of the word "hacking" was likely anything but. Clarence's computer shenanigans had been discovered. She extended her hand to me. "Tamara Gilroy."

Clarence hissed as I reached for her hand.

"A completely harmless handshake, cat. Nothing more

than a welcome to the neighborhood." With a twinkle in her beautiful eyes, she said, "I promise."

And for a moment, I caught a glimpse of a very different woman. One who stole my breath. I blinked and the motherly witch stood before me again.

What had she said? I saw her extended hand, which jogged my memory. She'd promised no harm.

Witches didn't lie. I wasn't sure where I'd learned that fact, but I seemed to recall it was a reputable source. Something about karmic debts or burdened souls. The specifics eluded me, but it was enough for me to ignore my poorly mannered sidekick and accept her hand, belated as the gesture was.

"Geoff Todd. It's a pleasure to meet you." And on some level, it was. I wasn't the only one living here, on this quiet street of humans, with the weight of otherness resting on my shoulders. Witches were more "other" than I was, in many ways.

Her welcoming smile turned to a grin. "I like you, Geoff Todd. Would you like to come in and have a cup of tea? No harm," she said, aiming a sharp look at Clarence.

I glanced at Clarence, now two feet behind me.

"The cat creature can come, too. He's very welcome." She leaned down so that she was nearly eye level with Clarence. "Even though he'd like to eat my liver."

Clarence sputtered. "*A* liver, not *your* liver." His head drooped low and his tone turned defensive. "I'm not a cannibal, just hungry."

She winked at him. "I thought there might be some human in there somewhere. Come inside. I think I have some chicken liver in the freezer I can heat up for you. And if not, how does beef heart sound?"

He stood to attention when she mentioned livers and hearts. In a much subtler whisper than was his norm,

Clarence said, "I might have been wrong about this one." Then he darted through the door and disappeared into the house.

Once we'd all gathered around the kitchen table—Tamara and me with herbal tea and Clarence with tiny cubes of medium-rare beef heart—I gave Clarence a look, hoping he'd be smart enough to use his company manners.

"He's fine," Tamara assured me. Her cheerful demeanor slipped slightly. "My own companion recently passed, and it's good to have a feline presence in the house again."

Clarence swallowed, then licked his lips. "Part feline."

Which made her grin again. "Yes, that's right. Might I ask what you've done? I sense only the one personality inside the bobcat body—and I assume that presence is you, Clarence."

That was news to me. And I suspected to my bosses— unless they'd had a witch take a look at Clarence. I hadn't even known witches could see such things.

Clarence picked up another cube and actually chewed this time, rather than swallowing it whole. He took his time, savoring the tiny piece of meat much longer than I'd have thought his greedy appetite would allow.

About what I'd gotten out of him myself so far: squat.

"To put your mind at rest, Geoff, if ever there was a soul before Clarence's in that body, it's long gone."

The hairs on the back of my neck stood to attention. How had she known?

Possession was a foul word, and the idea that Clarence had done such a thing—to any creature –had greatly altered my view of him. But if he wasn't sharing that feline body with another soul, did that make him the original owner? Creating a fully functioning body was magic unlike any I knew.

Tamara sipped her tea and watched me, seeing far too

much. My trouble alarms weren't ringing, but I suspected this meeting should end sooner rather than later.

"Clarence and I had planned to introduce ourselves as new neighbors and try to sneak in a few questions about your whereabouts the last few days."

"You weren't aware of my particular leanings," she said.

"The magical ones? No." And still wasn't entirely certain of them. She was a witch—but my intuition said she was perhaps something else as well.

"You might like to meet Hector when you have a moment, though best to try after sunset. He's more likely to open the door then."

Hector wasn't on the list. Was she saying Hector should be on the list?

"You think he might have relevant information?" I shared a glance with Clarence, but he shrugged.

"Oh, I have no idea. You'd have to ask him." With her face schooled to a pleasant neutrality, I couldn't tell if Tamara was concealing information or simply believed that Hector and I would hit it off.

When in doubt, courtesy was never amiss. "Thank you. We'll be sure to stop by."

"Perhaps not the cat, though he isn't truly feline, is he? I'll leave that to your discretion." She looked as pleasant as before, but something shifted. "Now, ask me your questions."

As I watched her sip delicately at her tea, it clicked. What I'd read as a certain pleasantness before was much more. It was balance. Tamara was in harmony, with herself, her environment, everything. And that harmony was currently being ruffled.

I set down my teacup and trained all of my attention on her. "We're here about the explosion in Sylvie Baker's house."

"Her shed." The correction was gentle, but firm. "The

explosion was in her shed. Quite some distance from the house."

That correction, that assertion of fact, made me very uncomfortable. I wanted to like this woman—this witch— but she was practically admitting some involvement, or possibly knowledge.

"I knew it," Clarence said. "The red hair is a dead give- away. Or it was, when you had it. Red-headed women have fiery tempers."

Tamara snorted, and that bit of ruffled energy I'd felt slipped away. "Nonsense. I have almost no temper at all. Be thankful, since I live within striking distance of your house, young man." She leaned forward, her elbows on the table, and said with a cheeky grin, "And the red hair was dye. This is closer to my natural color."

Her casual reference to Clarence as a "young man" surprised me. I didn't think Clarence was a young man at all . . . which brought into question Tamara Gilroy's frame of reference. I felt myself sinking deeper into a mystery I wasn't sure was related to Sylvie's problem, and probably wasn't one I should poke with a sharp stick.

Shifting gears, I let loose our money question, because Clarence and I needed to retreat and regroup. "Did you have anything to do with the explosion at Sylvie's house?"

Her pretty green eyes wide and the neutrally pleasant expression we'd seen on arrival firmly affixed to her face, she said, "I don't wish Sylvie Baker any harm, no harm at all."

Tuesday early evening

Clarence and I had ended our interview of Tamara as quickly as possible. I glanced over my shoulder at her picture-perfect front yard. A yard that held more magically useful herbs, flowers, and grasses than could occur by chance. How had I not seen it before now?

All we could get out of her was that she had no ill intentions toward Sylvie and that she wished her no harm. That and a very enthusiastic—even genuine, I thought—welcome to the neighborhood.

Since witches didn't lie, I took her comments concerning Sylvie to mean that she was in this up to her eyeballs, but that she didn't want Sylvie dead.

"Oh, she so did it." Clarence stalked in front of me at the very end of his leash. "She blew that shed to bits. Guarantee you, she did. Dye or no, red hair is red hair."

At least he'd waited until we were a few houses away before he'd started to lambast Tamara. "That beef heart didn't buy much loyalty, did it?"

"Give me a break. I may take bribes, but I'm pure where and when it counts, boss."

"Right." But there wasn't quite as much sarcasm behind the comment as there might have been in the past. "Why did you let everyone think you were sharing that body?"

He spat and hissed a bit. "That again? Leave it, Geoff."

And I did, because he wasn't going to say a word until he was ready. If my bosses couldn't get him to spill, then I had no chance. "What's with you and the red hair? You do know that's completely ridiculous, right? Someone's hair doesn't define their personality."

"That's what you say." He tugged on the leash, and I picked up the pace. We were just about to the house when he stopped suddenly, attention fixed on some point in the far distance. His voice uncharacteristically quiet, he said, "Red-headed women will always break your heart."

Then he picked up the pace again, pulling, darting, zigzagging, and generally trying to trip me. A completely normal cat-on-a-leash jaunt, as if he hadn't just shared an excruciatingly intimate detail.

Trying to fill the silence, I mentioned Hector.

Clarence paused. "He's been here a few years; that's why he didn't make the list. You think we should bump him up?"

"No, but I do think we should swing by and introduce ourselves the first chance we get. I don't think she mentioned him casually."

As we passed Sylvie's house, a curtain twitched, and not five seconds later she emerged waving. "Mr. Todd—Geoff!"

Clarence and I crossed the street again to join her. I hoped she was distracted enough by recent events that she missed his left-right-left check for oncoming traffic.

She frowned, giving Clarence a curious look. "Did your cat . . . No, never mind. How are you?"

Since I hadn't recently lost my shed to an explosion . . . "I'm fine, but more importantly, how are you doing?"

She didn't look like she'd recently suffered a traumatic event. She was wearing a pretty dark blue dress with white embroidery, the thin straps showing off her tanned shoulders. She had beautiful shoulders. I lifted my gaze several inches.

"About that . . ." She clasped her hands in front of her, twisting them this way and that—but no explanation followed.

Clarence butted me with his head.

Nudging him away with my toe, I made a note to thank him later. "Ah, thank you for having me over last night. After you, ah—"

"Passed out?" The twisting stopped, and she touched her fingers to her forehead, effectively covering her face.

"No, not at all. After you retired for the evening, I had a short chat with Bobby." I must have been moving in the right direction, because her hand lowered and she peeked at me. Encouraged, I continued, "He didn't have much of value to add. But I had to check him off the witness list."

Her hand fell back to her side as I spoke, and I swallowed a sigh of relief.

"Does that mean you have other potential witnesses?"

Ghosts were one thing, but witches another. And outing Tamara was simply not an option.

"We have a few leads, and we're working on a list." All true.

She cocked her head and smiled curiously. "We?"

Clarence smacked me with a paw—claws extended.

I nudged (kicked) him away. "Me, sorry. Just a turn of phrase."

"Like the royal 'we'?" She grinned, flashing her dimple again.

"I guess. So, I was thinking, when you have a moment, maybe we could sit down again and you could tell me about your husband's work history?" No need to mention I, via my talking and typing cat, had pulled Bobby's work history already. She might be able to fill the gaps, primarily how his completely above-board-appearing employment was in any way shady.

"Sure, I'd love that." With a wry smile, she added, "And maybe no wine this time. I'm a bit of a lightweight."

"I'd probably drink more than a few glasses of wine if someone had done that kind of damage to my home." I couldn't quite manage to say "explosion" or "bomb." The words were too close to the reality, and it seemed wrong to say them in her presence.

"At least you didn't catch me drinking tequila or whiskey. That's a sight. Trust me." She shook her head, but now I was curious to know what exactly tequila or whiskey did to her that constituted "a sight." She licked her lips. "I'm off to work now for a few hours, but if you'd like to get together this evening . . . ?"

"You're working already?" Modern women, independence, and some other related, liberated-type thoughts flashed through my head, and I realized perhaps I'd misspoken. "Sorry, yes, this evening would be lovely. What time?"

She bit her lip, but her eyes crinkled. "Eight. Your place?"

"Absolutely, I'll see you then."

"And Geoff, thank you—for last night."

"It was entirely my pleasure."

She smiled and her dimple made yet another appearance. I was developing a strong affection for that dimple. "You are an odd combination of the traditional and modern man, Mr. Todd."

"I'm not sure if that's good or bad. Maybe give me a hint?"

She laughed—but didn't answer.

As I watched her walk back to her house, Clarence said, "It's good, Geoff. Trust me on this one."

I wasn't taking romantic advice from a talking (and frequently lecherous) cat, even one who'd just revealed the presence of a heretofore hypothetical heart.

15

Tuesday evening

A message from Lilac was waiting for me on my answering machine.

"This is Lilac. Is this an answering machine? Geoff, you really need to get a cell phone. Anyway, I've given it some thought, and . . . Well, just come by today if you can. I canceled my appointments, so I'm free. I'll be here until about seven. And, you know, bring the cat."

Encouraging? Maybe not. But there was at least a possibility of acceptance stashed in that message. Canceling appointments might be an indication of a personal, professional, or existential crisis. But it might also just be her working through some complex variables, or even making time for an important client.

That last one wasn't very likely, but I could hope.

"She's fine."

"What?"

Clarence heaved a huge sigh. "You had that look, like

someone had drowned your favorite kitten. Lilac sounded fine on the message."

"Please stop with the drowned kittens. And by the way, drowning any kitten would be bad. The favorite part is overkill."

"Got it, boss. So call Lilac already."

Right. I picked up the phone and dialed the number from memory.

She picked up after one ring. In a breathless voice, she said, "Geoff, thank . . ." But her voice trailed away as if the connection was poor or the phone far away. But then, much more clearly, she said, "You're coming?"

Caller ID. It was baffling on so many levels how such a simple device could alter phone etiquette so significantly. "Yes. Clarence and I can swing by within the hour, if that works for you."

"Uh-huh. Ah, hurry." And she hung up.

I held the phone in my hand and stared at it. I was not a fan of this abruptness.

"She said 'bring the cat' on the message. I heard her." Clarence's ears pricked forward, and when he looked at me, his pupils were huge. "You can't leave me at home."

We'd just been out, and yet the thought of a trip had him so overstimulated that he could barely think straight. If I didn't find a way for him to constructively occupy his time, all that bottled-up energy and excitement would explode into a mushroom cloud of mischief.

"I'm not leaving you, but if you do anything to push Lilac over the edge, I might dropkick you into traffic."

Clarence sauntered to the garage door, all feline grace and confidence, unruffled by my hollow threats of violence. "It wasn't me that had her screaming, was it? That was all you, Mr. Retired Death."

He was right, but that didn't mean I had to like it—or

speak to him on the ride to Lilac's shop.

When we arrived, the store windows were dark. It looked like she'd locked up early. Not completely shocking, given her stated intent to cancel all appointments for the day, but I'd expected the retail store to still be open, like it had been when we arrived last time.

When I tried the door it was locked, but I caught a glimpse of movement from inside. I rapped sharply on the glass door a few times.

Within seconds, Lilac was at the door unlocking it and motioning us inside. She looked around outside with a furtive, panicked glance then locked the door behind us.

Clarence had gotten this one wrong. He'd said Lilac was fine after listening to her message, but the woman standing in front of me was not fine. Her skin was pale and clammy and her eyes red-rimmed.

"You have to help me." She gasped and then held her breath, clearly trying not to break down into tears.

"Of course. Whatever we can do." I didn't know whether to hug her like a child or hold her hand.

Her eyes met mine and she crumpled into a sopping mess, tears streaming down her face.

That answered one question, at least. I removed a newly laundered handkerchief from my shirt pocket and handed it to her. It was always appropriate to offer a lady in distress a clean hanky, whatever the year.

Thank goodness for Mrs. Feldhaus, my cleaning lady, because I hadn't yet mastered the art of laundry or ironing.

"Boss." Clarence's voice came from the back of the shop, eerily disembodied in the dark room.

"Just a minute, Clarence."

Lilac bawled into the scrap of linen for several seconds, then started to hiccup, then drew several ragged breaths. She wiped her eyes and clutched the damp hanky tight in her fist. "I think I'm in trouble."

"Boss," Clarence called again.

I turned to reply, but stopped when I saw the haunted look on Lilac's face. Her eyes were locked on the same dark corner where Clarence had disappeared. "Everything okay back there, Clarence?"

"I'm not so sure about that, boss. I think we have a problem."

Holding my hand up as I left, I said, "Wait here."

Lilac didn't move a muscle. Even her eyes remained fixed and staring.

The difference in light between the front and back of the store necessitated a slow approach to allow my eyes to adjust. When I arrived, I found Clarence on the sofa that was pushed against the back wall. Next to him was the slumped figure of a man. But for the disturbingly absolute stillness of his body, he appeared to have simply stopped to rest his feet and fallen asleep.

He was large. Though it was difficult to gauge with certainty, since he was seated, I estimated him to be taller than me, and I was well over six feet. He was also easily fifty pounds heavier, which made me cautious as I felt for a pulse. "He's dead."

Clarence turned his head, and the light caught his eyes, making them glow. "Boss? I don't think that guy was ever alive."

16

Tuesday evening

"What?" Lilac called from the front of her store. "What does that mean, never alive?"

We needed some light. To try and handle a situation involving a body in the dark, whether dead or never alive, was ridiculous. I scanned the front of the store and discovered that Lilac had hung curtains made of a deep teal velvet.

"Lilac, draw the curtains."

"Oh, right. I should have thought of that." She hurried to comply but then stopped. "So we're not calling the police?"

"Get those windows covered, then we'll discuss it." I knelt next to Clarence and the body, then quietly asked, "What is it?"

"I'm not sure, but my nose isn't getting human smells," Clarence replied.

As close as I was now, I could see his nose flare as he scented the air.

"And there's blood, but no metallic scent. It's not like any human blood I've smelled." He crept closer and ducked his head in the vicinity of the body's head. "There. As best I can tell in this light, it looks like blood—but it's not."

A trail of dark fluid had run from the side of the creature's head and dripped onto his white collar. For a nonhuman creature, one that had possibly never been a living being, he'd been well dressed: a crisp white-collared shirt tucked into a pair of slacks, a conservative tie, and the shoes looked expensive and newly shined. My imagination said tattered clothing and the smell of the grave was more appropriate for what appeared to be a human facsimile.

My imagination was an idiot. "Earlier, when I checked his pulse, he was cold. If this just happened—"

"Oh, he'd still be warm. This guy's no guy." Clarence reached out a paw and gently tapped an arm.

Lilac approached, stopping a few feet away with her arms crossed tightly against her body. "The windows are covered."

"If we turn the lights on, can anyone see inside the store?" From where I was crouched next to the body, it looked safe enough. She hadn't covered the glass door, but only the front of the store was visible through it.

She shook her head, but then her gaze fell on the big guy and she started to tear up again. "I didn't mean to k-k-kill him." She lifted the much-used hanky to her face. "I'm not a killer. I don't even squish cockroaches or spray wasps. I do catch and release for scorpions!"

It took a second for me to make sense of cockroaches, wasps, and scorpions, mostly because I could barely understand her with the hanky pressed to her nose and covering her mouth. "Right. I'm sure there was a good reason for what you did."

She pointed at the man. "His eyes glowed."

Clarence made a hairball-hacking noise.

Since that could be either a prediction of cat yak to come or Clarence laughing hysterically, neither of which was a situation Lilac seemed equipped to handle, I stepped between the two and made a shushing motion behind my back. "His eyes glowed, so you felt the need to defend yourself."

She frowned at me like I was a lunatic. "No, of course not. I didn't hit him until he tried to strangle me. I just thought you should know that his eyes glowed—since you were saying how he wasn't alive. Or the cat was saying that."

"Clarence," Clarence said in a huffy voice. "The cat's name is Clarence."

She craned her neck so she could see behind me, then stepped to the side. "I'm so sorry. Of course, Clarence." But then her gaze fell on the man-creature who wasn't bleeding real blood, and she started rambling. "I wasn't entirely sure . . . and murder . . . and the police . . . you know . . . so I called you, Geoff. I . . . That man . . . his eyes . . ." She stood up straight and closed her eyes. When she opened them, she said much more calmly, without signs of hyperventilating, "He tried to strangle me, and that's when I bashed him over the head."

I looked at the hulking giant on the couch and then at Lilac. He was so much bigger than her that "over the head" had been the side of his head. Even so, I was having a hard time seeing how she'd had any chance at all. "What exactly did you hit him with?"

Lilac pointed at a small sculpture on the ground a few feet away.

"Do you mind getting the lights, Lilac?"

She nodded and moved to the back wall several feet away, and seconds later the room filled with light.

Now I could easily see the blood and hair on the small statuette lying near her desk. When Lilac came to stand next to me, I asked her, "What happened *before* he tried to strangle you?"

"Boss, you better hurry up," Clarence said. "Something's happening with the body. It's getting warmer."

Warmer? Waking up? Coming back to life? Maybe the thing wasn't killable. We needed an expert.

"Phone book. I need a phone book." I scanned the room, but didn't see one. Lilac was rooted to the spot, unmoving, possibly unhearing, so I raised my voice. "Quickly, Lilac. I need your phone book." I had a hunch that I knew one person who still had a landline, a listing in the white pages, and an idea what exactly was propped up on the sofa, looking almost human.

Lilac ran to her computer. "Who am I looking up?" She gave me a helpless look. "I don't have a phone book."

That computer class at the local library couldn't start too soon.

"Look up Tamara Gilroy." And I watched Lilac's fingers fly across the keyboard.

Seconds later, she said, "I've got it."

Tamara answered on the third ring, sounding neither surprised nor put out that I had telephoned her without being given her number. "How can I be of assistance, Geoff Todd?"

I racked my brain, trying to remember any tricks or hidden traps when trading with witches. Nothing came to mind, so I relied on her honesty. "I have a problem and need advice. Is there any harm to me or mine in asking you for that advice?"

"None, though I may not have an answer for you, naturally." She sounded mildly amused.

"I have a recently terminated, cold body that doesn't smell human and is rapidly heating. Are we in danger of harm?"

Without hesitation and with no hint of amusement, Tamara replied briskly, "Quickly, dowse it in water. Blessed, if it's available. The entire shell."

Shell? What was this thing?

I turned to Lilac. "Blessed water?"

She nodded but continued to stand still and stare at me. I gestured for her to hurry, which resulted in a relieved look followed by a flurry of action as she ran to retrieve water. When she returned, she held a small flask.

I rubbed my neck as I reported back to Tamara. "I only have a small flask, six to eight ounces." Lilac shook the half-empty flask. I gritted my teeth. "Perhaps half that, but the woman I'm with is a practitioner of . . ." I scanned the walls and then her desk. I looked at Lilac as I said, "Hoodoo?"

She looked to the ceiling and shrugged.

My gaze continued to travel over the collection of charms, crystals, and herbs scattered around the store. "And Wicca?"

She nodded agreement.

"Yes, she's confirmed, hoodoo and Wicca." I'd noticed the hodgepodge of philosophies when I was first in the shop, but now that I would be relying on Lilac's skill as a practitioner in one of those arts, her flexibility was somewhat more concerning.

In a resigned tone, Tamara said, "Young people will experiment. Go on, then, hand me over to your practitioner."

Lilac reluctantly accepted the phone. When she put it to her ear, she flinched and then began to reply at an increasing rate. "Yes. No, not by me. Lunar." She glanced at the body. "Still looks normal. Okay. Tap water? All right." She looked at me and pointed to the front of the store. "Fetch all the sea salt, all of it. Our blessed water isn't any good."

Then she disappeared into the bathroom. The sound of running water emerged. When she returned, she was carrying a bucket filled almost to the top, the phone tucked between her ear and shoulder. "Okay. I'll do that. Yes, I promise. I'll call you right back."

The seconds ticked by as Lilac performed a quick blessing of the water as, I could only assume, she'd been instructed by Tamara. When she'd finished, she looked up and screeched.

The body was emitting a red glow, something we'd missed, since Clarence had abandoned the body to watch the blessing. Now that I was paying attention, I could feel the waves of heat pulsing off it.

"Help me," Lilac called, lifting the bucket. "This is heavy, and we need the water in here evenly spread across his body."

Clarence followed us but stopped a good ten feet from the body. "I hope you know what you're doing."

Lilac frowned. "Well, I hope this Tamara person knows what *she's* doing." She looked at me. "Ready?"

I nodded and lifted the bucket up and over the now-crackling body. She tipped and guided the bucket, while I slowly traced a path from head to feet.

"Wow! Would you look at that?" Clarence crept a few feet closer. "He's turning black, just like that burned-to-a-crisp chicken you tried to bake the other day, Geoff. And he looks all crunchy and stiff." Clarence let loose a whistle.

Then the creature's eyes popped open.

C larence and I screamed like little girls.

Lilac gaped. When the creature blinked, she let out a little "eep" and then said, "Quick, if you have questions, you have to ask now, while he's vulnerable. Tamara said you might get a few answers from him." She hustled in the direction of the bathroom, bucket in hand. She called over shoulder, "I have to make more blessed water."

Death didn't have a physical body. Not one that could be hurt. But as a retired death, I was human—just as susceptible to having my neck broken, my heart ripped out, or the breath squeezed from my lungs as the next guy.

And that was why it took several seconds to realize the creature hadn't moved: because I was consumed by fear for my mortal body.

"Psst." Clarence poked me with a claw. "You gonna say something?" He poked me again. "You know, boss, I think his crunchy exterior has him trapped."

A whooshing breath left my chest. "Right." I inched closer. "Ah, who sent you?"

Its lips moved, making them crack and sending charred bits flying. "My creator and master."

"Who is your creator and master?" It seemed a simple enough question when I asked it, but the working of the creature's stiff jaws with no resulting sound indicated otherwise.

Finally, it said, "My creator and master."

"Simple, straightforward questions," Lilac called. She was busily stirring sea salt into the bucket. "Sorry, I forgot that part."

How much simpler did it get then the name of the guy he was working for? Simple . . . "What do you want?"

"The stone."

I shared a glance with Clarence, but he shook his head.

"Okay, charcoal head," Clarence said, still several feet away. "Let's say we want to help you get the stone. What does it look like?"

With great effort and a lot of flying charred bits, the creature turned its head to look at Clarence. "You have the stone?"

The hopeful note in its voice reminded me of a needy puppy, desperate to please. I wasn't about to lie, even if the thing wasn't human and served an ill purpose. "No. We don't have the stone. What is the stone?"

The caked material around its eyes—something I was now convinced was not actually skin—crumbled as he blinked. "The stone is."

I waited for the punch line, and it never came.

Lilac approached with the bucket, once again full of water. "He asked me about the stone. When I told him I didn't know what the heck he was talking about, that's when his eyes glowed."

"And then you bashed in his head," Clarence said.

Lilac shot Clarence a censure-filled look. "No, then he

tried to strangle me and *then* I bashed his head." She let out an exasperated breath. "Look, I'm not sure he'll be able to talk once I dump this bucket, so hurry up and ask your questions. I don't want to wait and have something freaky happen. Like an explosion or him setting my couch on fire."

A fire, especially of the magical variety, seemed like a bad idea in this cozy little shop, so I hunted for my next question. Why Lilac? That was the most pressing one, so I asked him.

"Li-lac. The girl has the stone?" Again with the puppydog hopefulness.

With sympathy, I replied, "No, the girl—Lilac—does not have the stone." I was beginning to have an inkling what exactly this creature was. And if I was right, the kindest course of action was to complete the process of disassembling him. "Why are you here?" I modified my question, quickly realizing my error: "Why would the girl have the stone?"

"The girl has the stone. Or"—the creature paused and blinked—"the girl has knowledge of the stone." He repeated the phrases as if they'd been memorized, each time pausing between the different options.

He'd been programmed to believe those statements were fact, and I suspected they were the basis of his goals.

"Your goal is to retrieve the stone. Or"—I paused, emulating him—"gain information about the stone."

"Yes." I'd swear the creature was pleased that I'd gotten it right.

Since he, or it, liked its archetypes, I tried one of my own. "Death protects the girl. The girl has no stone." I looked at Lilac. "You don't know anything about a stone, right?"

She looked around at the store. "Except for the crystals here in the shop, no. Certainly not one that would have some Neanderthal man threatening me. I buy them in bulk."

The creature's eyes darted this way and that, like he

couldn't decide where to look or whose response to process. Finally, his charcoal-encrusted gaze settled on me. "Death protects the child. Not the girl, the child."

Before I could puzzle that one out, Clarence said, "Dowse the thing already!" He groaned. "The girl, the child, the stone —this walking, flesh-covered tin can can't help us. Geoff, it's programmed to think in terms of archetypes. It's a construct."

"Yeah, I think you're right, Clarence," I said. "Not that I've ever actually seen one, but signs do point that way. And I do think we've gotten about as much out of him as we can." I picked up the bucket at Lilac's feet.

"Wait, I do have one more question." Clarence leapt up on the couch, no longer concerned the incapacitated creature would suddenly regain its mobility. "Who's the child?"

The creature blinked. "The child is the false owner of the stone."

"Right," Clarence said in a disgruntled tone. "Ask a stupid guy a pertinent question, get a stupid answer." He shook one front paw and then the other, dislodging stray bits of charred creature, then hopped off the sofa. "Okay, folks, let it rain."

It took a total of three full buckets of blessed water before the construct was completely neutralized. The creature's warm, parched skin absorbed each bucket. The sofa and the body should have been a soggy mess—but the creature was bone dry and the sofa only damp around the edges of the corpse.

After the third bucket, its skin started to crack and break apart. Within seconds, it had crumbled to ash. Just add water, then get ash. *That* was magic.

Lilac stared—at her ruined sofa or the piles of ash or simply the place where the creature had once been and was no longer—then said, "I guess it's a good thing we didn't call the police. Now what in the goddess's name is a construct?"

Clarence shook his head. "Don't look at me. Geoff's better at explanations."

"Not it" was one of Clarence's favorite games. After several weeks, it shouldn't bother or surprise me. But there was "shouldn't," and there was reality. "Fine," I said. "A construct isn't real, in the sense that it is the thing it appears to be. It's more a shell of something real." Eyeing the bruises that were darkening on Lilac's very fair skin, I added, "Though obviously its physicality is not in question."

She lifted a hand to her throat but didn't touch the skin there. "So a construct is a man that's not a man. Looks right, almost talks right, but isn't made up of the right stuff."

"She's better at this than you." Clarence plopped down on the ground and started to groom himself. I only hoped he wasn't consuming ashy bits of our visitor as he did so.

He suddenly spat repeatedly, like a foul taste coated his mouth. I couldn't help but laugh.

"So, about this construct?" Lilac asked.

"Right. They're only capable of completing a simple task or two, and take an enormous amount of skill and power to create. Or so I hear." I shrugged. "I've never come across one before. But if you consider that it arrived, interacted within this reality somewhat like a human—enough to pass inspection by a casual observer—and pursued its goal while maintaining a veneer of humanity, that's power."

"You're forgetting his eyes glowed." Lilac shivered. "That's hardly human."

"But that only happened after you refused to give him what he wanted," I reminded her. "You wouldn't tell him where the stone was."

"I didn't know where it was. Or even what stone he meant."

"Well, exactly." I gave her a sympathetic look. "He couldn't complete his task. I'm guessing that's when he reached out to his master to check-in—and the eyes glowed."

Clarence cleared his throat. "Anyone else wondering how little buck-ten here managed to take down the big, bad, nasty construct?"

We all turned to the small sculpture still lying on the floor. I'd seen the blood and hair, but only as I approached it did I see that the statue was an oddly proportioned, hunched figure with a grotesque face: a small gargoyle, possibly iron.

The bits of blood and hair that had been stuck to it were conspicuous by their absence, replaced by a fine, ashy powder that speckled the carpet next to it.

I reached for it, but stopped myself. "May I?" I asked Lilac. When she nodded, I picked it up. It felt solid, hefty. It was a good weapon, but not something I'd expect to bring down a construct when wielded by a small woman. "And you didn't use any magic? You just hit him—it—with the gargoyle?"

"Magic, right." Her freckles stood out sharply against her pale features. "No. No, Geoff, I did not use any *magic* when I whacked the intruder in the head with my bookend." Then she sank onto the nearest non-ashy surface, which was the edge of her computer desk.

I considered another alternative. "The gargoyle was a gift?"

"Yes," Lilac said, surprised. "From my father. How did you know that?"

"Just a hunch." I placed it gently on her desk. "Maybe keep it handy for the next few days, just until all this has settled down."

She considered the gargoyle for a moment, then hopped down from her desk and retrieved it. "Done." She rubbed her collarbone, not touching the bruises.

"We're supposed to call Tamara and update her, right?" I asked, thinking, *Who better to have a healing salve on hand?*

"Yes, that's right." Lilac squeezed her eyes closed and wrinkled her nose. "I forgot. I was supposed to remind you about your date. I forgot, what with all the blessings and the dousings . . . and everything."

"Date?" I pivoted slowly to Lilac. "She called it a date?"

Tired, pale, and certainly overwhelmed by all that she'd seen this night, Lilac still managed a teasing smile. "She did. You're meeting your neighbor, right?" She glanced at the wall clock. "In fifteen minutes?"

"Yeah, I have to go or she's going to get to the house before me." Which would be mortifying. Maybe I should get one of those cell phones—just for emergencies. "Can you handle the call to Tamara?" When Lilac nodded, I said, "Tell her I'll come by in the morning, if that suits. I'd like to offer my thanks in person. Oh, and ask her about something for your neck."

Tomorrow gave me a little time to come up with the appropriate bouquet for a witch. I didn't want to accidentally offend her, even if she claimed she didn't have a temper.

"Will do. And Geoff? I'm really sorry about the way I acted earlier. You know, with the cat, with Clarence." She smiled, making her beautiful in a way that runny mascara and red eyes simply couldn't diminish. "I'm glad I called you and not the police."

"I'm honored to have been of service." I poked Clarence in the ribs with my toe.

"Yeah, what he said. Happy to help." Then Clarence muttered, "Even if you can't remember my name."

As I buckled Clarence into his carrier, he said peevishly, "If I didn't know better, I'd say she was a redhead."

"What's your issue with Lilac? Just because she calls you 'cat,' you have a problem with her?" I didn't comment on the fact that, given her green hair, she certainly could be a redhead. And with her pale skin, deep blue eyes, and the faint dash of faded freckles across her nose and cheeks, I'd say odds were almost even on blonde or redhead. But best not to taint Clarence any further against Lilac. She'd done a smashing job in a difficult situation, something that Clarence would surely recognize—at some point.

The entire ride home, I had to listen to Clarence moan about the evils of redheads. Even as we turned onto our street, he still wasn't done.

It wasn't until he caught sight of the flashing red and blue lights in front of Sylvie's house that he stopped complaining.

"Slow down!" Clarence wailed from the backseat. "I can't see anything. I always miss all the best stuff."

"If you don't hush, I am going to do something—I don't know what, but something—that you will not like. Put aside your obsessive need to be entertained for two seconds and think about Sylvie." I whipped into my drive and jammed the gear shift into park.

"I'm sorry, boss. I'll wait in the car while you check on her." His tone was contrite enough for me to pause for a split second before I slammed my car door shut and consider if he might actually be experiencing remorse.

As I jogged across the street, I made up my mind: I was buying a cell phone tomorrow.

A police officer parked at the curb stepped out of his vehicle.

Since he looked like he was going to stop me, I preempted him. "I had a date this evening with Sylvie Baker, the home-owner. Can you tell me if she's all right?"

"She didn't call you?" He took out a small pad and pen from his pocket.

Ignoring the implication that she would have if she wanted me here, I gave him a chagrined look and said, "I don't have a cell phone." As his eyebrows rose, I lied, "On me. Just lost it."

The officer clicked his pen. "Your name?" He glanced at his watch and scrawled the time on the pad.

"Geoff Todd." I even spelled it for him.

Once he'd written down my name, address, and landline number—since I'd "lost" my cell phone—he escorted me to the front door. "Hey, Ernie," he called inside. "I've got a Geoff Todd here."

Ernie must have given me the stamp of approval, because the officer waved me through and then returned to his parked cruiser.

Sylvie and a tired-looking plainclothes cop who didn't look nearly old enough to be out of a uniform were sitting in the living room.

"Geoff, I'm so sorry about this evening." Sylvie stood up, and I couldn't help an appreciative look. Her dress wrapped around her neck—called a halter dress, if I remembered correctly—and cut into a deep V in the front. It was a pattern of blues and reds that I was sure would normally flatter her skin, but she was pale as a ghost.

I hadn't a clue if she'd smack me or thank me, but I closed the gap between us and pulled her close.

She leaned into me, wrapping her arms around my back and pressing her cheek to my chest. The delicate scents of vanilla and cinnamon tickled my nose. I rubbed her back, wishing that whatever the hell had happened to upset her hadn't.

She took a deep breath and then stepped away. She had a little more color in her cheeks. "Thank you."

For coming over when I saw the police? For comforting a distressed woman? That was just what one did, when—

Ah, just the thing to do. I cleared my throat. "What happened?"

Sylvie's gaze drifted to the detective.

"Ms. Baker interrupted a burglary."

My blood pressure shot through the roof. I felt the tips of Sylvie's fingers on my arm. If I didn't want to give the impression of being a hothead—and I wasn't one—I needed to offer a reasonable response.

While I worked on that, Ernie gave me the basics: "Ms. Baker did exactly the right thing. She avoided confrontation and immediately called the police." He turned to Sylvie and said, "You kept yourself safe, which is really smart thinking."

"I don't think he knew I was here," Sylvie said. "I usually park in the drive, but I decided just today to start parking in the garage." She rolled her eyes. "Like that turned out to be safer."

"Did you see him?" I asked. When she shook her head, I added, "But you're sure it was a man?"

A wrinkle appeared between her eyes. "No, I just assumed. I got the briefest glimpse of his—or her—back and just focused on getting out of the house. I left through the back door, went around the opposite side of the house, and over to your place, actually."

"But I wasn't there," I said grimly.

"No. I hope you don't mind, but I waited in your back-yard until the police arrived and retrieved me."

Ernie piped up. "We searched the entire house before Ms. Baker returned home. And you still don't think, Ms. Baker, that anything is missing?"

Sylvie shook her head. "Not that I can tell, but I'll have a closer look and let you know." She saw Ernie and I share a concerned look and rolled her eyes. "Tomorrow. I'll have a closer look tomorrow. I'm spending the night at a friend's house, per your recommendation, Detective Nelson. Though

I really don't think that's necessary." She looked around the room and seemed angry for the first time since I'd arrived. "This is my *home.*"

Ernie flipped his notepad shut and said his goodbyes. I didn't get the impression he had much hope of catching the intruder, not unless someone in the neighborhood had seen more than Sylvie and could provide a description of a car or the burglar.

Once he was gone, I tried to gauge her state of mind. The woman who'd wrapped her arms around me looking for support seemed to be gone. It was just as well, since I had some troubling information for her. I would have loved an excuse to wait—she'd only just learned about Bobby—but the events of the evening seemed likely to be related. Superficially, perhaps not, but this many crimes in such a short time, all happening to a small group of people—it simply couldn't all be coincidence.

She looked down at her red and blue outfit. "All dressed up and nowhere to go." Shaking her head, she turned to the kitchen. "Whiskey?"

"Ah, sure. I thought you didn't drink much whiskey. Or tequila. I distinctly remember you warning me that those particular beverages do not agree with you."

She stretched up on her tiptoes and pulled down a half-full bottle of whiskey from the back of a kitchen cupboard. "Desperate times." She lifted the bottle in a sort of toast.

She retrieved two glasses, poured us each a stout measure, and then sat down at the kitchen table. Gesturing to the seat next to her, she said, "Now, Geoff, why is it I get the impression you have something you need to tell me? I thought I was the one with the adventurous day."

I hesitated, stalled by taking a sip of her excellent whiskey, and then set the glass down. I took another sip and swirled the liquid around in my mouth. It was possible, though not probable, that the events at Lilac's store were unrelated. I hated that the greatest connection between the events, besides timing, was me.

She placed both forearms on the table and leaned toward me. "Spit it out."

My breath stopped. She was gorgeous, with her determined expression, her daringly beautiful dress, and a glass of whiskey in her hand. She could have asked me just about anything, and I'd have told her. "It could be completely unrelated. Probably is unrelated."

She tilted her head, waiting.

"Right. I just came from Lilac's shop. Ah, Lilac is a medium whose help I've been seeking to resolve some problems."

She quirked an eyebrow.

"I have a ghost spying on me, and I don't know when she's around. It's disconcerting." My face warmed.

"She?" Sylvie's eyes crinkled, and she took a sip of whiskey. "Go on."

"That's not the important part."

"Oh? But it is interesting." She grinned, her dimple making its first appearance of the evening. "You're blushing."

I leaned back in my chair. "Okay. She might have had a certain fascination with some of my daily routines. That's all I'm saying. I asked Lilac to help with a detection system and, if possible, some kind of ghost repellant to keep them away entirely."

She nodded. "That seems a reasonable enough request."

Maybe she and Lilac needed to meet, because I wasn't sure Lilac would agree even after the events of the evening. Something she'd said about spiders and bugs had me doubting she'd shifted her position.

"Tonight, right before a meeting I had scheduled with

Lilac, someone attacked her." I watched Sylvie's face closely. "Some*thing* attacked her."

Concern clouded her face. "She's all right?"

"She is. But the . . . man who attacked her was looking for an item."

Sylvie tapped her finger against the table. "You think there might be a connection between the explosion in my backyard, the burglary tonight, and this attack on your friend."

"No, not necessarily. There's no real connection other than their proximity in time."

"And you."

I winced. "Yes, and me."

She swallowed some whiskey then licked her lips. "So, what was Lilac's attacker looking for?"

"A stone, if you can believe it."

Not even a glimmer of recognition crossed her face. "Hm. Like a diamond?"

"I have no idea. It wasn't very forthcoming."

Her eyes narrowed. "What exactly was *it*? And what else are you not telling me?" She pinned me with her beautiful brown gaze. "I've had a rough day, so don't even try to pull the wool over my eyes. I am *not* in the mood."

I crossed my arms. "You're sure you want everything? I don't know if that's a great idea, especially since you have had an especially rough day."

She thumped her empty glass on the table. "Geoff Todd, spill."

So I did. Everything. The construct, Clarence, my former profession. I even told her about Tamara, her friendly (I hoped) neighborhood witch. And all the while she listened silently, not asking questions, making accusations, or voicing doubts.

Given how poorly my recent revelation with Lilac and

Clarence had gone, I was on edge when I was done. I had just enough time to remind myself that Sylvie was no Lilac before a knock on the door interrupted us.

And that was that. I got no response from Sylvie about my various earth-shattering disclosures, just a gentle shove out the door.

Wednesday morning

A text. That was what I got from Sylvie the next day.

The modern world had its foibles, and texting was certainly one of them.

After enduring a night of Clarence's complaints (did I know how stuffy that car was while he'd waited for me?) and curiosity (what exactly had her face looked like when I mentioned the talking cat part?), I'd rolled out of bed bright and early and bought myself a cell phone.

The first number I'd called was Sylvie's, but I'd gotten a recording saying to leave a message. So I did. I'd asked how she was, which felt odd, since she couldn't reply. Then I'd given her my number, explaining that I'd picked up a cell phone this morning, and asked her to call when she was free.

And she'd replied with a text.

"Well, what does it say?" Clarence looked at the phone in my hand.

"What does what say?" I stuffed the phone in my pocket as I'd seen others do, except it felt large and awkward. I should have ignored the salesperson and gone with the smaller phone.

"The text message you just got from Sylvie. You're the cell phone newbie, Geoff, not me. That was a text message."

How did he know? Of course, the only person with my new number was Sylvie. The smell of perfectly crisped bacon brought my attention back to the stove. "Bacon?"

"You can't distract me with crispy pork fat. What did she say?"

"So, no bacon." I shoveled all three pieces on my plate, then cracked an egg in the pan. Granola and yogurt weren't cutting it today. Not when I'd skipped my usually early breakfast for an emergency phone-shopping trip.

"Whoa, wait now. I didn't say no to bacon. The answer is always yes when the question is bacon, but I still want to know what she said."

Maybe he'd have some insight. Clarence was much more acclimated to the modern world than I was. Decision made, I retrieved my phone and read the message aloud. "'Thanks for last night.' But she spells it with an x. And then, 'Talk later today.' That's it."

Clarence picked up his front paw and started to groom himself.

My frustration bubbled over after approximately five seconds of whisker grooming. "So?"

He swiped his paw across his face again. "So what?"

Frustration wasn't my favorite emotion, but it was becoming a close companion since I'd met Clarence. "So, what does it mean?"

"Where's my bacon?"

"Too hot to eat." I already knew what a greedy kitty and a sizzling piece of bacon meant, and it was bad news.

He proceeded to groom his whiskers.

I stalled by retrieving one of the small plates reserved for

Clarence's use and cutting up a slice into smaller pieces, but it was still hot when I set the plate down on the ground.

"Was that so hard?" He gulped two small squares and then yowled.

Rubbing my ears, I said, "Yes, Clarence, it was."

He spat and hissed, all the while keeping a close watch on his bacon lest I take it back. When his mouth had cooled, he asked, "Was there an exclamation point?"

"What?"

He stabbed a small piece of bacon on the tip of a claw, but managed to pause before chomping it just long enough to say, "The text, Geoff. Was there an exclamation point?"

Did that matter? But I retrieved the phone from my pocket and checked. "No. No exclamation point. What does that mean?"

He stabbed another piece of bacon and shoved it into his mouth—then shrugged.

"You don't have any better idea than me." I rubbed my twitching left eye, because that was what I got for taking advice from a cat. The morning stretched out before me like a long wait at the dentist's office. "When we're done with breakfast, we need to stop by Tamara's."

"Sure thing, boss."

Visiting a witch—one I was convinced was something more—had its own set of traps and hazards. Tamara seemed pleased enough with the bouquet I'd brought her. I'd landed on odds and ends from my own garden, because I thought that was the most genuine expression of gratitude I could make. But to be welcomed into the witch's kitchen and find a gaggle of women congregating—that made the hair on the back of my neck stand up.

"Good morning Lilac, Sylvie. Am I late?"

"What he said. Are we late?" Clarence tugged on his leash, pulling toward the table and the scent of food.

I'd tried to convinced Clarence to stay home, but I'd have tried harder if I'd known Sylvie was going to be here. A glance showed her looking surprisingly composed for a woman who'd just heard a cat speak for the first time.

"Lilac and Sylvie called earlier and asked if they might come by for coffee." Tamara indicated the pot. "Would you like a cup?"

"Ah…" The feeling of being ambushed made me edgy. Who knew what was in that coffee pot? Who knew what they'd been talking about? What did women usually talk about? Had I come up? And if so, in what context and what light? I waited for those warning bells in my head to clang with a loud warning, but they were silent.

Tamara waved a hand dismissively. "No harm, Geoff, I promise. We're just sorting out some of the problems that have cropped up recently, and sometimes that's best done with like minds."

"And I'm not like-minded."

Tamara shrugged. "You're a man."

Sylvie frowned. "Geoff's not like that."

Nodding, Lilac said, "Right. Geoff's cool."

Flicking my gaze between the two women, I wasn't certain whether to be thankful they were defending and including me, or concerned that I'd somehow unknowingly let down my gender. When I saw Tamara's amusement, I landed on my answer. "Thank you. I appreciate your support."

Now I had to wonder what concerns Lilac and Sylvie had expressed about me before my arrival that Tamara felt the need to unite them in their acceptance of me. I was betting it had something to do with my previous employment.

Maybe my occupation as death—one of the deaths—had been better kept under my hat.

Tamara clasped her hands together. "Now, if you ladies are ready to proceed . . . ?"

"Hey! What about me?" Clarence had kept a low profile up to that point. Which was admirable, no matter the limited duration.

"You're welcome as well, Clarence, so long as neither of the ladies objects."

My concern was mostly for Sylvie, since she'd only just heard about Clarence, but she looked disconcertingly serene.

Tamara gestured to her right at the seat next to Lilac and placed a cup of coffee on the table for me. Clarence helped himself to the seat closest to Sylvie.

She didn't even lift an eyebrow as he leapt into the seat and assumed a regal pose. Maybe he'd display his Sunday-best manners, if he had any.

Once I'd settled into my chair and enjoyed my first sip of Tamara's truly exceptional coffee, I asked, "What conclusions have you reached?"

All three women turned to look at me, and Tamara said, "You're the common denominator."

Since Sylvie and I had come to the same conclusion the previous evening, her pronouncement shouldn't have carried any particular weight. And yet it did.

My alarm bells weren't ringing, but an uncomfortable feeling grabbed hold of me. "You don't think I'm responsible? The attack on Lila, the explosion at Sylvie's, the break-in . . . I didn't have anything to do with them."

"No. No, that's not what we mean at all." Sylvie frowned at Tamara. "Is it? *I* didn't mean that."

"Of course not." Tamara took Sylvie's hand, gave her fingers a quick squeeze, then let go. "I don't think he's responsible for any of those things. And I most certainly would never accuse Geoff of the bombing." She paused, sipped her coffee, then said, "I did that one."

20

Wednesday mid-morning

Somehow we'd traveled from me being at the center of the nefarious goings-on to Tamara Gilroy, friendly neighborhood witch, bombing Sylvie's shed.

The theme music to *The Twilight Zone* played in my head. Seconds passed before I pinpointed an external source: Clarence. He whistled the tune as he gave Tamara the evil eye —or the cat version of it. I nudged his chair leg with my toe, and he stopped.

"Why would you bomb my house?" Sylvie asked in a small voice.

Tamara and I both said, "Your shed."

I raised both hands. "But I had no idea it was Tamara." It didn't make any sense. The crime *or* confessing. "Why would you do such a thing?"

Clarence tapped the side of his head with a paw, which I translated as the sign for a crazy person.

"I'm not crazy, cat. I was trying to protect Sylvie." Tamara turned to a dumbfounded Sylvie and said, "You have the most beautiful aura." Then she squinted. "Usually. Either way, you certainly didn't deserve our kind of trouble. You still don't, even if your aura is a little muddled now."

"Muddled?" Sylvie's cheeks were stained a bright pink. "My aura is not muddled. I'm pissed off. That's righteous anger you see clouding my aura."

Lilac didn't comment, but her eyes were huge as she watched the unfolding scene.

Tamara said, "Our world is a difficult place. I know it's hard to believe, but I truly was trying to protect you."

"You can talk about 'our' world all you like, but *I* don't blow up my neighbors' sheds," I said. "I moved here because it was a quiet neighborhood." No need to mention my multi-stage, months-long plan for quietly reintegrating with humanity. That plan was up in smoke, in part due to Tamara and her neighborhood bombing shenanigans.

"Well, I'm not talking specifically about you, Geoff, more the supernatural crowd in general. It's a bad bunch to run afoul of. I figured whatever they'd been looking for in her shed wouldn't be a problem anymore if I blew up the building a little bit." A look of consternation crossed Tamara's face. "I'm much better with magic. The result was a little bigger than I'd planned."

A startled laugh escaped Lilac. Her hand flew to cover her mouth. "I'm so sorry. It's just all so ridiculous. Who in the world blows up something 'a little bit' to help someone?"

Sylvie's eyes narrowed. "No one, that's who. Nice, normal, *sane* people call the police. Or just let their neighbors know there's a problem."

"Ah, and there's the flaw," Tamara said. "I'm not normal, not in the way you mean. I'm not human. No one who has magic is fully human—or what you'd most likely label normal. And I was trying to keep you away from a particularly unsavory element within the not-entirely human crowd."

Tamara's argument took a curiously circuitous path to a less-than-logical conclusion—in my mind. In her own, it seemed to make perfect sense. And I still wasn't getting any particular read off her that made me believe she was dangerous.

Perhaps I was giving my intuition too much weight, but it had held me in good stead as a soul collector.

"Who was searching her shed and for what?" I asked. "And why did blowing it up seem like the best answer when you could have, as Sylvie mentioned, just warned her? Or retrieved whatever it was this undesirable element wanted from her shed."

Sylvie shot me a censorious look. "You believe her?"

"I want to hear her story," I countered.

"Quite sensible." Of course Tamara would say that, especially if Clarence was right and she was as nutty as a fruitcake. "As for the explosion, that was my attempt at discretion."

I set my coffee cup down. "Tamara, as much as I'd like to believe you have a pure heart in this matter—"

"Oh, I never said my heart was pure. Much as I admire Sylvie, I also don't want the wrong element on our little street. It's shaping up to be a wonderful little spot. Have you met Hector yet?"

My left eye started to twitch. I pressed my thumb to the corner and tried to remember why exactly I'd retired. The difficulties of collecting recently departed souls weren't nearly as complex as human life or supernatural life among humans. Maybe they'd take me back.

But I couldn't go back, and that left going forward. "Please explain, Tamara, how blowing something up is discreet."

"Arson and man-made explosions *are* discreet when you're talking about magic." She winked at me. Turning to Sylvie with a more serious expression, she said, "Your ex-husband was involved in dubious business dealings with that auto shop he ran. I thought they'd blame him and his connections, since some of his business records were stored in your shed. I am sorry to have worried you, but I thought this would keep any real harm away from you."

"Wow." Clarence stood up with his front paws on the kitchen table. I snapped my fingers at him, but he ignored me, focusing all his attention on Tamara. "Just wow. There's a twisted logic there, but just wow."

Sylvie wasn't looking convinced. Curious, but not convinced. "How would you even know someone had been in my shed?"

"I have a . . . let's call it a magical eye on the street. Like a neighborhood watch."

Clarence snorted. "Sounds like spying on your neighbors."

"No, cat, I do not spy. It's not as if I have a Snow White mirror that shows me the goings-on of the neighborhood. If I did, I'd know who broke into Sylvie's shed. This is more like a detection grid."

"His name is Clarence," Lilac said with a frown. "Your detection grid beeped like my home security system, except magically, so you knew zone five—or whatever you call Sophie's house—had a magical visitor. Is that about right?"

"Not exactly. If we're going to use a security system comparison, it's like I've got the windows and the doors wired, but no motion sensors. If someone uses magic to breach a building, I know. If any magic anywhere in the neighborhood set off alarms, then we'd be in a pickle." Tamara gave me a pointed look. "Geoff's house, for one, is teeming with activity."

"My house?" I asked, surprised. Then again, why not my house? Clarence, for one. And the various ghostly visitors. And the little bit of whatever magic I had that allowed me to act as unwilling medium. "Ah, never mind. I do see your point."

Lilac twisted her green hair up in a knot with a look of intense concentration. "So, if I understand this correctly, someone broke into Sylvie's shed using magic. Is that right?"

"Exactly right," Tamara said. "Because Sylvie follows good common sense and locks her shed, my alarm was tripped when they used magic to fiddle with the lock. I checked it out, but I couldn't find anything magical inside or anywhere else on the premises. I suspected they were done, but then they broke in again. That's when I decided it was only a matter of time before Sylvie interrupted one of their attempts. I'm sorry I was right about that, dear. But that's why I decided I needed to take preventative action."

"Someone broke into my shed *twice*? And that's only what you know about." Sylvie looked dismayed by the thought. "I might as well get rid of my fence and leave the stupid shed open—assuming I even replace it. There's practically been a parade through my backyard."

Lilac leaned forward with a concerned look. "Once this is over, we can cleanse your yard and even your house, if you like."

"Thanks, sweetie." Sylvie touched Lilac's hand. "I might take you up on that."

"Why come clean now?" Much as I liked to believe the best in people, people—supernatural or not—were a self-interested lot. And while my trouble meter might not be flashing warning signals, something was up.

Tamara turned her attention to Lilac. "The attack on Lilac."

I looked at the marks on Lilac's neck. She raised her hand

self-consciously, covering the bruises. The marks had darkened to a dusky purple overnight.

"But if you're responsible for the shed and not the other incidents, then . . ." Lilac's forehead creased. "I don't understand. What does Geoff have to do with the two crimes?"

"I suspect the answer to that question is timing." Tamara lifted the coffeepot. "More coffee, anyone?" When no one replied, she refilled her own cup.

Sylvie pulled a leather-bound book out of her purse, along with a pen. A fountain pen. I hadn't seen one in a long time. She flipped the book open, rifling past pages with notes and sketches until she came to a blank page. "When was the first break-in?"

Now here was a woman I understood. Sylvie, unlike Lilac when I'd introduced Clarence the possessed cat, had calmed immediately when presented with a task.

"Two weeks ago, yesterday," Tamara said. "And the second was a week after that."

Sylvie tapped the end of her pen against the paper. "They like Tuesdays?"

"Apparently," Tamara said.

Sylvie sighed. "Which was why you blew up the shed on Monday." With a mixture of confusion and disappointment on her face, she asked Tamara, "Couldn't you have come to me and explained everything? Maybe we could have found what they were looking for, and . . ."

"And given it to them?" Tamara asked. "Destroyed it? Which bombing the shed was supposed to accomplish without involving you."

"Or discussed it so that *I* could decide," Sylvie said acerbically. "Whatever this item is, it's apparently my property. Okay, back to the time line. Tamara bombs the shed, at which point I've already met Geoff—"

"Then I meet Lilac," I said.

Sylvie tipped the end of her pen at me. "You meet Lilac."

"And Lilac is attacked," Lilac said with a quirk to her lips. "So maybe there's speculation by the baddies that this item they can't find is now being handed off."

I thought back to my initial attempts to use the internet: so much information, so many bad sources, so much false data. "Or maybe this is more about knowledge. Let's say I'd fessed up to Sylvie right away that I was a retired soul collector, if she had a supernatural question, she might ask me."

"And we already know that if *you* have a question about the supernatural," Lilac said with an amused look, "you head to the phone book, which, in this case, led you to me."

We all looked to Sylvie. She dropped her pen and spread her hands out. "What? I have no clue what it is that these people want."

Lilac snapped her fingers. "I forgot to mention, in all the hubbub—you know, getting strangled, thinking I'd killed a man, not a construct of a man, and then meeting a real witch." She took a breath. "The stone. Remember, Geoff, I told you—the burned construct guy asked me about a stone."

"Hm," Sylvie said. Then her eyes widened and a dismayed look crossed her face. "Oh. Oh my." She looked at us with a guilty expression. "I think I know what stone."

21

"There." Sylvie pointed to a rock in her garden. "I can't believe it's still here." She looked at me, Lilac, and Tamara. Tamara had won a short reprieve, but I doubted Sylvie would so easily forget or forgive the incident. Tamara had shown an appalling lack of judgment—by human standards, in any event.

I'd detoured by my house to drop off Clarence. He'd been relatively quiet during the meeting, and when I'd commented, he'd complained that hunger was making him lightheaded and a single piece of bacon didn't go very far.

Completely absurd—the lightheaded part, not the bacon part. One could never get enough bacon. Then again, he had agreed to munch on kitty kibble till I could get home and cook up something more appetizing. Clarence normally had very strong and decidedly negative feelings about kitty kibble, so I knew he was ravenous.

The ladies had been kind enough to wait the three or four minutes it had taken for me to run across the street and unlock the front door for Clarence.

And now we were all staring at a rock.

A decorative rock in a garden.

"It's beautiful?" Lilac said tentatively.

And it was. It was an unusual combination of green and red. I could pick it up with one hand, but it wouldn't fit in my palm.

"Dragon blood jasper, Australian in origin." Tamara looked at Sylvie. "Are your people from Australia?"

A tiny wrinkle appeared between Sylvie's eyes, "I can't be sure. My mother's family is from Italy. My grandmother's from the UK, but she would never say who Dad's father was. It was a huge family scandal at the time."

"Really?" Lilac wrinkled her nose. "I mean, I get it's different now, what with sperm donors and adoption and all the options available—but people have always had affairs."

"Certainly. They just didn't get caught, not without society frowning mightily," Sylvie said. "Or so my mother used to say when she wasn't feeling charitable toward my grandmother."

"Hm." Lilac shrugged. "My mom was a hippie and a single mom. Different worlds, I guess."

Tamara patted Lilac on the shoulder. "Different times."

We all turned our attention back to the rock.

"You're sure this is *the* stone?" Lilac asked. "It looks pretty innocuous."

"So does your gargoyle," I reminded her.

Tamara looked at me curiously, so I briefly explained: "Lilac knocked out the construct with an iron gargoyle her father gave her."

"Ah. Keep that close until we've sorted this all out," Tamara said, echoing my sentiments from the night before. When Lilac agreed—and even produced the little guy from the depths of her monstrous purse to prove she already was —Tamara returned her attention to the rock. "Now, about this stone—Sylvie, do you know where it comes from?"

"My grandmother left me some things. A few boxes, some furniture. It was right after I moved into this house. There wasn't a place for everything, and it was also a difficult time. I'd finally changed my name back after the divorce because I'd foolishly kept Bobby's name." A hint of bitterness crept into her voice, the first sign I'd seen of any real animosity between her and her ex. "I'd also waited so long to buy my own house, so that was quite emotional for me, though in a different way. And then to have my grandmother pass . . . It was all so much in such a short time. The furniture was a reminder I didn't need."

Something about that story wormed its way into my brain and set tiny alarm bells ringing—but which part?

Sylvie stared at the shed. I thought for a second that she might cry, but she turned back to us dry-eyed.

Lilac looked uncomfortable, like she didn't know where to put her hands. "I'm sorry. About losing what your grandmother left you." Then she shot Tamara a disappointed look.

"Thank you. Although I think I still have what my grandmother most wanted to leave me." Sylvie looked back at the rock. "It was in one of the drawers. I thought it was pretty and that it would be a nice complement to Clive, so I put it in the garden."

"Clive?" I asked.

She pointed to a garden gnome with a shovel. She'd placed the rock near the shovel.

"Oh! That's cute." Lilac grinned. "And I'm not one for gnomes usually, but he's a good one."

The two women shared a moment of admiration for Clive, which broke the emotional tension somewhat.

"I suppose I should retrieve it." But Sylvie remained firmly planted a few feet away. "I'm reluctant to touch it. It sounds silly, even to me, since I didn't have any problems moving it from the shed to the garden."

"That's not strange at all. Magic is part perception and part belief." Tamara pointed at me. "This one knows. His job was dependent upon convincing the dead to *believe* they'd passed. Without an acceptance of death, the soul lingers."

I nodded. True.

"So now that I know it does something, it can actually do that thing. No, that doesn't make any sense." Sylvie clasped her hands together. "Never mind. I just need to retrieve it, and then we can stash it somewhere safe, right?"

The question was rhetorical—she was already leaning down to pick it up. I looked away after getting an eyeful of her heart-shaped derriere. I hadn't noticed the capris and figure-hugging T-shirt earlier, but they were impossible to miss now.

By the time I'd distracted myself from a variety of less-than-gentlemanly thoughts, Sylvie was standing, but without the rock.

She said to Tamara, "And you're sure you don't know what it does?"

"I'd have told you, I promise," Tamara replied. "I can't detect any magic at all. If I could, I'd have found it before when I searched the property."

Except the burglars would have likely made it to the rock first, if that were the case. They at least knew to look for a stone. Rock, stone, basically the same thing.

Sylvie assumed a skeptical expression. One could hardly blame her for losing faith in Tamara. Blowing up someone's house, even if it was technically an unattached outbuilding, tended to have that effect.

"Witches can't lie." I volunteered the information, in hopes it would set Sylvie's mind at ease.

Tamara tilted her head. "Don't lie. We can, but the consequences are unpalatable."

She wasn't helping, but I couldn't do much else. So I

nodded as if "unpalatable" signified a significant deterrent. "There you go."

Lilac let out an exasperated sound and snatched the rock from the ground. "There, all done. It's totally fine, right?"

As she held the rock, a change came over her. She closed her eyes and her expression was transformed. She looked like a little girl lifting her face to the sunshine after nothing but days of rain. Then a single tear slipped down her face.

When she opened her eyes, she let out a breath and swiped at the dampness on her cheek. "Your grandmother loved you so much." Then she blinked and looked confused. "I have absolutely no idea what just happened. I swear, nothing like that has happened to me before."

Sylvie took the rock. "Well, you're right—my grandmother and I were very close. As a child, I adored her. She was such a kind woman. She worked as a nurse most of her life, and she was incredibly popular with her patients." Sylvie smiled, but looked miles away. "She used to say, 'Be kind to the living, because you never know what grudges will last beyond death.'" Sylvie smiled, but it was tinged with sadness, and her dimple stayed out of sight. "Of all people, she would have known."

"This is your grandmother who could talk to ghosts," I said. Sylvie looked at me in surprise, so I added, "You mentioned her before, when we first discussed Bobby."

Her face cleared. "That's right." She hefted the rock in one hand then transferred it to the other. "So is that what this is? A message from my grandmother?"

"Hm. I don't think so," Tamara said. "At least, that's not all it is, because there's little value to a third party in such a message." She wasn't looking at Sylvie when she answered, instead shooting speculative looks at Lilac. "What was it you said about your business? That your psychic readings were more therapy with a dash of intuition than fortune-telling? Maybe you've been focusing on the wrong skill set."

Lilac's pretty blue eyes widened, and she shrugged. "I've always considered myself more of a medium than a psychic, but a girl has to keep the new age shop lights on."

"We'll chat." Tamara looked at the stone again. "Later."

Lilac nodded. "Where to stash it, that's the question we need to be focusing on. I don't suppose you have a safety deposit box, Sylvie?"

"Actually—"

A chirping noise sounded from the vicinity of my pocket, and then a split second later, I felt a vibration. Once I was certain my heart hadn't stopped, that I'd merely received a text message, I retrieved my phone with the intent of shutting the thing off. "Apologies."

Before I hit the power button, I realized that the only people with my number were present. I swiped the message open.

I have the cat. The cat for the stone, instructions to follow.

Lilac peered over my shoulder and read the message aloud. "The cat? Oh, heavens above and hell below, the baddies have Clarence."

22

Wednesday midday

"We can't give them the stone. For all anyone knows, it's some kind of magical nuclear weapon." I regretted my words instantly. Thankfully, my reflexes were fast enough to catch the stone before it hit my stained concrete floor.

We'd convened at my house, because it seemed only sensible to verify that Clarence was gone. After a thorough search of the premises, we confirmed that he wasn't trying to steal porn online or wallowing in my bed in an attempt to make it smell better and cover it with bobcat fur—his two favorite pastimes. He wasn't anywhere in the house or yard.

Sylvie looked at her hands in horror. "Oh . . . oh . . . rats! I am so sorry, Geoff." She pointed at the table when I asked what I should do with the hopefully *not* nuclear rock.

Which left Lilac, Sylvie, and I staring at the rock on my kitchen table, waiting for the one person who might have a clue to return.

Tamara had gone home to retrieve some supplies. When

we'd asked if it might not be wiser to move to her house—
where all of her supplies and equipment were located—she'd
declined. Until she could do a cleansing, she didn't want visitors, especially in an emotionally charged situation. After the
big "I was the bomber" reveal in her kitchen, she said there
were some bad vibes in her home. My words, not hers. She'd
made it sound much more technical and complicated.

Rather than twiddle our thumbs, I figured we could make
some kind of headway, so I asked the first question that came
to mind. "How did the kidnappers know about the stone?"

Sylvie shrugged. "Maybe they knew my grandmother . . .
knew about the will . . . Uh, maybe, I don't know, someone
close to my grandmother told them. For all I know, a ghost
told them."

"Oh, I see. This is a good question." Lilac tapped the table
impatiently. "It wasn't in the will, not directly. And you didn't
even know about it, Sylvie."

"Okay, a ghost, then?" Sylvie didn't look convinced.

My gut said not, but it couldn't be ruled out. "Maybe, but
I'm thinking it has to be your family. Perhaps a—"

Sylvie's humorless laugh interrupted me before I could
ask about her relatives. "Certainly not my mother or father.
They both thought Grandmother was more than a little
looney. My poor grandmother." She reached toward the
rock, but stopped shy of touching it. "It's just a bundle of
trouble. Nuclear magic or not, I'd be glad to give it to them to
save your friend."

"Bad idea," Tamara said from the living room.

All three of us jumped.

Tamara placed a bag on the kitchen table next to the rock.
"Apologies. I didn't mean to startle you. The front door was
unlocked." She gave me a censorious look. "Sylvie, without
knowing what it does, I think it unwise to relinquish it."

"Right, but it's not yours, is it?" Sylvie said—and we were

back to the decision Tamara had already made, namely blowing up Sylvie's shed. "And it's also not your friend who's being threatened."

A diversion seemed in order, so I grasped at the weak lead we'd come up with in the witch's absence. "So, Tamara, we were discussing the possibility that the kidnappers were members of Sylvie's family."

"Mr. Crispy said something about the child being the false owner of the stone," Lilac said. "That points to a family connection, too." She bit her lip and nodded, her eyes wide. "I was paying attention, you know, in between blessing the water and freaking out."

"It's an heirloom of sorts," I said, "and who knows about family heirlooms but family? It has to be someone in your family, Sylvie."

Sylvie looked confused, tired, and frustrated. She didn't argue with me, but she didn't agree, either.

"That seems reasonable," Tamara said. "While you sort through your suspect list for a family connection, I'm going to scry for a location. My success with pendulums and location scrying has been wildly variable, but if it works, well, then it's well worth the bit of time it takes." She pulled out a well-worn map of Austin and spread it on the table. "Before you start, I do need—"

My phone chirped, the sound dropping ominously into the warmth of my kitchen. When I didn't move fast enough, Sylvie dug the phone out of my back pocket and swiped open the message.

She let out a sigh of relief. "They don't know that we've found it. They're giving us three hours to find the stone and deliver it. They'll send the address immediately before the drop time."

She handed the phone back to me. After scanning the message for any hint of a clue, I moved to pocket it again.

"Wait, what's the number?" Tamara asked.

I looked but couldn't see what she meant. "There's no number."

Lilac grabbed the phone. "There's always a number, even if it's one of those weird short numbers." But after swiping open both messages, she frowned. "There's no number. There's nothing. It's just blank."

"Magic," Tamara replied. "We can't use the text to track them. But I'll still try the old-fashioned way. I do need something of sentimental value to Clarence."

Annoyance flared like indigestion in my gut. "He's a cat. He doesn't have sentimental trinkets."

Also, I hadn't a clue what he valued, and that made me angrier than it should.

"What does he enjoy doing the most?" Sylvie asked.

"Watching dirty movies, stealing my credit cards, and eating." I shook my head, frustrated that there must be something, and I didn't know what it was.

"Hang on." Lilac jumped up and ran out of the kitchen. She returned carrying a soft, fuzzy blanket I'd picked up for Clarence on a whim. It would appear at odd places throughout the house, like the window where he watched the birds or in front of the TV.

"Perfect. Thank you, Lilac."

"I noticed it earlier when we searched the house. There's a lot of cat hair on it, so . . ." Lilac handed the blanket to Tamara. "I had that thing happen again, like with the rock. Anyway, I think it's one of the few things you've given him without being asked . . ."

It was. The only thing.

Tamara wound a small piece of the blanket around a tiny charm that hung from a thin chain. I had the ridiculous thought that Clarence would be upset someone had snipped a piece from his binkie, and I laughed.

Sylvie rubbed my back. "He's going to be fine. And if we can't find him, we'll just give them the stone." She flashed Tamara a stern look, daring her to voice an objection.

The objection came, just not from Tamara.

No, no, no, no trade. Bad people.

"Bobby? What do you mean bad people?" I asked, trying and failing to find some visual evidence of him.

Trade stone, dead cat. Dead, dead, dead cat.

My left eye throbbed, keeping time as he continued to chant, *Dead cat, dead cat, dead cat.*

"Bobby. Stop it. I understand." I pressed my thumb to the corner of my eye.

Dead cat, dead cat, dead—

"Bobby!"

Lilac winced at my tone, but pointed to a spot near the stove. "I think he's there."

"You can see him? Hear him?" I asked. Bobby wasn't a powerful ghost, and so it was difficult for him to make himself seen or heard. But some psychic ability was required to pick up the signals the ghost was sending out. I had a touch of that skill, hence my ghostly stalkers. But I hadn't been sure till now that Lilac did. The more powerful the ghosts—and the ghost's signal—the less powerful the medium need be.

And then there was Clarence, who just blew them all away. No medium skills required.

Lilac shook her head. "I don't ever see or hear them. I just get a feeling that they're present." She looked completely comfortable with her "feeling" about Bobby, unlike her psychometric experiences today.

"Suspect list? Family connection?" Tamara prodded. "I can't concentrate with the racket." Tamara turned her attention back to the charm that dangled over the map. The tip of the charm moved, vibrating.

I blinked, peering closer. The charm she'd used to anchor the snip from Clarence's blanket was a tiny unicorn. Its little horn was pointing toward the map.

Tamara looked up and caught my eye. "It makes me happy. Now shoo."

Once we were in my office, basically a converted bedroom, I called out to Bobby.

Here, here, here. Baaaaaad people. No trading. Dead cat, dead cat, dead cat.

"Stop." In a softer tone, I added, "Please. Sorry, Bobby, I get it now." I sighed. There went any hope that he'd been confused earlier. "Bobby says that trading with the kidnappers is a bad idea. That they're bad people." I ran a hand through my hair. "He's quite persistent in his belief that a trade would result in Clarence's death."

Sylvie paled and then dropped down into my desk chair with a solid thud. "Does he say why he thinks that?"

Killers. Kill Lilac.

"No, Bobby, they didn't kill Lilac. She's here." I pointed to her, and she waved to a space near the window.

Kill Lilac. Bad people. Lilac nice.

When I recalled that Bobby didn't have a great grasp of tense, I got his point. "I see. They *would* have killed her. They tried to kill her."

Bobby didn't argue, just repeated that they were bad people. And... *Kill Bobby.*

"Bobby, are telling me you remember who killed you? That these people, the ones who hurt Lilac and took Clarence, that they killed you?"

Kill Bobby. Kill Bobby. Kill Bobby. And then he wailed and his chant changed. *Kill Sylvie. Kill Sylvie. Kill cat.* And each time he repeated "kill," he grew more agitated.

"Bobby—" Sylvie's breath caught, and she had to start again. Her eyes shiny with emotion, she said, "Do you know *where* Clarence is? If these people might hurt him, we have to go and get him. Make sure he's safe."

Don't know. And he wailed, a mournful, horrible sound.

"Um, he says he doesn't know, and he's pretty torn up about it," I said. "He also thinks Sylvie and Clarence are in danger." Then the obvious answer fell on me like an anvil. "Damn. Ginny. Ginny would know. Maybe not where he is, but if the kidnappers grabbed Clarence here in the neighborhood, I guarantee she'd know who did it." I whacked the wall in frustration. It made my palm hurt, but it also made me feel better. "I'm an idiot."

"Okay, for the sake of expediency, we'll agree you're a total numbskull." Lilac moved to meet my eyes. "But tell us who Ginny is and how she can help."

Figuring discretion was key, I said, "Another ghost who's grounded in the area. She's more cognitively intact than Bobby. Sorry, Bobby."

Bobby started to moan and wail again. This must be what it sounded like when ghosts cried. It made my heart hurt and my stomach churn.

"It's going to be fine, Bobby. We're going to sort this out. We'll get Clarence back and keep Sylvie safe."

Kill Clarence. Kill Sylvie.

"What's he saying?" Sylvie looked fragile and anxious, a disconcerting sight in a woman who'd seemed more like a bold, brightly colored piece of stoneware than translucent porcelain.

"He's worried." I turned my attention to the spot near the window, feeling foolish for addressing a blank wall. "No,

Bobby, that won't happen. I promise to do everything I can to keep Sylvie and Clarence safe."

The anguished, ghostly sounds stopped. Since I doubted my assertions, however confidently uttered, had comforted him, I suspected he was gone. "Lilac?"

She shook her head. "Gone. So far as I can tell."

"Tell me you've managed to retrieve something useful from the ghost." Tamara stood in the doorway. She exuded that unsettled, out of-harmony feeling that I'd occasionally felt from her otherwise very serene presence.

"No luck scrying Clarence's location?" I asked.

She motioned for us to follow her back into the kitchen. "It's possible he's here in the neighborhood. I can't see much here or in any of the other supernatural hot spots in Austin." Approaching the table, she indicated several places on the map that were shaded a light gray. "There's simply too much interference. That's also why I have trip wires set up for certain things here—like the trespass alarm that was tripped at Sylvie's."

"We live in a supernatural hot spot?" My left eye started to twitch.

"Why do you think you were drawn here? And me, and Hector—have you introduced yourself to Hector yet?"

I shook my head. Because no, I hadn't introduced myself to the mysterious Hector, what with the complete absence of any free time since I'd learned of his existence. And no, I didn't think I'd moved here because it was a supernatural hot spot. Just the opposite. I'd moved here because I thought it was a nice, quiet street.

"I'm sure there are others, but they haven't been as neighborly as Hector," Tamara said.

"Hector . . ." Sylvie pursed her lips as she thought. "I know, I met him on Monday! Right after the explosion. He was the large black man with the unusual hazel eyes. He was lovely, so kind. He offered to build a new shed for me if I bought the supplies. But he was just there for a moment and then gone again."

"He took one look at me and retreated." Or so it had appeared to me at the time.

"It's the daylight," Tamara said. "It puts him in a terrible mood. He's not usually out and about until later. Hector's more of a night owl." Tamara pulled out a scrap of paper and printed a number on it. She pushed the little scrap closer to Sylvie. "Call him when you're ready. He wouldn't offer if he didn't mean it, and he'll create a beautiful building for you. One that will be much harder to blow up."

And now my curiosity concerning the mysterious Hector had trebled.

"And we're sure this Hector, whoever he is"—*what*ever he was—"isn't involved?" I didn't think it appropriate to bring up the bombing again, but if Tamara was capable of blowing up a shed, what were all these other supernaturals who were hanging around in my "quiet" neighborhood capable of?

"No. Impossible." Tamara's implacable tone had me half convinced, but there was clearly something supernatural going on with the man. If he was a man. "Although if we don't come up with a reasonable solution soon, we might want to stop by and see if he has something to help us through the upcoming meeting."

I glanced at the clock.

"Two hours left," Sylvie said. "What now? Ginny?"

"I can try, but I'm not sure how to get in touch with her." I asked Tamara if she had any thoughts.

With a brisk nod, Tamara said, "Now we consult some toads."

24

"Ah . . ." But I didn't have a ready reply to ghostly communication via toad consult.

Clarence might have been right when he said Tamara was crazy. Intermittently, she'd put on a good show of sanity, but it looked like the cat was out of the bag. Or perhaps the toad?

"Oh, fun!" Lilac clapped her hands. Immediately her enthusiasm died. "I'm so sorry. That was insensitive. Of course I'm worried about Clarence, but"—her eyes lit up again—"toads!"

And now everyone was insane. Or I was the slow kid in the class, the one with spitballs stuck in his hair. "I guess I missed that seminar. How does one consult with toads?"

"Oh, no." Sylvie looked faintly queasy. "This doesn't have anything to do with entrails, does it? I don't think I could kill a toad." Her color fled, followed by a warm flush.

"Why would we kill a toad?" Tamara looked confused and a little concerned. "We're going to talk to one."

Because that made so much more sense. Maybe I was overreacting. In the grander scheme of things, talking toads weren't all that shocking a concept. After all, my housemate was a talking bobcat.

Tamara stopped rummaging in her bag, looked up, and said, "If I can find a sociable one at this time of day. It wouldn't be a problem at all if it were dusk or later." Then she returned to her bag.

"And what exactly will this toad tell us? Assuming we can find one." I blinked at the marble Tamara pulled triumphantly from her bag.

"I thought I had one in here, though I did pack this bag some time ago." She rolled the large marble in her fingers. "One should never be without a bit of gold, or in this case, a small golden ball."

Lilac grinned and held out her hand. "May I?"

Tamara handed her the marble. "The toad won't tell us anything. If we're lucky, he'll get the word out to your helpful ghost, Ginny."

"Helpful" wasn't the way I'd describe Ginny, but now seemed a poor time to mention her faults.

Sylvie watched Lilac roll the ball in her hand with a hypnotic fascination. But then she shook her head and turned to me. "You seem certain Ginny must have seen something, but if she has such a watchful eye on the neighborhood, then wouldn't she know we're looking for her?"

"Ah, about that . . . she might be specifically avoiding me. It's possible you could get her attention if I were gone, but she's also shy. Sort of." I wasn't about to explain my role as Ginny's unwilling evening peep show. And I couldn't in good conscience mention her tragic past and how that might have influenced her ghostly interactions with people.

Tamara finished mixing together several powders from the vials in her bag, then dipped her pinky in the mixture and tasted it.

Once I'd recovered from my choking fit, Tamara, who was still alive and showing no signs of poisoning, said, "Now, who has some tall grass and a little shade?"

After some discussion, we determined Sylvie's backyard the best option, since she'd been overdue a mow back before the explosion and had postponed it due to debris. The wildlife that had been driven away by the blast were proving surprisingly resilient and were already returning to her little back garden, so she thought we might have some luck.

Tamara stuffed the rock in her satchel with Sylvie's approval. With her traveling magic bag in hand, she led the way across the road to Sylvie's.

She pulled the prepared mixture from one of her deep pockets and retrieved the small gold marble from Lilac. Then she found a nice shady spot, rolled the golden ball, and murmured a few words.

Then we waited.

After what seemed an awkwardly long moment of silence and no action, Tamara picked up the ball and handed it to Lilac. "Give it a try. Just a gentle roll in the grass. I'll do the rest."

With a shrug, Lilac bent down and rolled the ball as instructed. Tamara whispered a few words that I couldn't make out—perhaps in German?—then we waited.

Not five seconds later, a sleepy, slightly peeved-looking toad hopped our way. Sylvie, Lilac, and I all stared. Then Sylvie nudged me in the ribs. "It's a toad. I can't believe that worked."

Her whisper barely reached my ears, so I hadn't a clue how Tamara, several feet away, heard her, but she said, "I'm concentrating over here."

So we all watched, waiting for the toad to say or do something. At least, I was.

Tamara took the powdered mixture and, after tapping small amounts out, made a circle around the toad. She looked at me and shook her head. "He's a conduit, Geoff. He's not actually going to speak. He doesn't have vocal cords. And could you think a little quieter?"

Could I think quieter? What did that even mean? And since when could witches read thoughts? But I tried as best I could to turn down the volume of my thoughts without actually knowing what that meant, and watched as the toad jumped out of the powder ring and then back in, and then again twice more.

And that was it.

Nothing else happened, but Tamara looked quite satisfied with herself. Turning to me, she said, "It's not all bright lights and explosions."

Lilac nudged me. "She's here—I think. *Someone's* here."

Ginny flickered into sight. "The toad said you wanted to see me. This better be good, because you're not my favorite person right now."

Tamara might have made the toad-enabled call, but Ginny only had eyes for me. I, on the other hand, was having a hard time pulling my attention away from the mysterious toad. I didn't think I could ever look at the odd creatures the same way again. But then he hopped away, leaving me to face Ginny.

Ginny scanned the group. "There are a lot of people here."

Unlike Bobby, Ginny was powerful enough to make herself seen by non-mediums. And she was clearly making that effort now, because Sylvie looked right at her. "Thank you. Oh, thank you so much, Ginny, for coming."

Ginny flickered, a sign that her emotions were already running high. "Do I know you? I don't think so." She pointed a finger that encompassed all three women. "No talking." Her eyes narrowed and her finger returned to Sylvie. "But especially you."

Like a ghost with a crush wasn't bad enough, now I had a ghost with a crush who was jealous. I motioned for Lilac, Tamara, and Sylvie to step back a few feet, and they quickly complied.

"Ginny?" I said, with an effort at a charming smile. It was about as difficult as taking my shirt off was when I'd known someone was watching. As a soul collector, my job had been difficult, yes, but it had also been straightforward. I'd been honest, because to do anything less was to undermine the trust between oneself and the soul to be collected.

Deception was a skill, and it appeared I was woefully out of practice.

She stopped glaring at the women and turned her attention to me, but she didn't look much happier.

"Thank you for coming," I said, trying to be casual and charming and nonthreatening all at once.

I suspected I just looked out of sorts, because Ginny crossed her arms with a grim look. "You sent a toad after me. Hard not to hear the message."

"Yes." I glanced at Tamara. "I'm new to, ah . . . toad messages."

Ginny snorted. "Of course it was the witch. I should have known." Ginny used two fingers to point at her own eyes, then Tamara's, then her own.

The message was clear enough: like everyone else on the block, Ginny was keeping a close eye on Tamara.

Tamara didn't look terribly concerned, so I pushed forward with our agenda. "I have a few questions for you about what's happened in the neighborhood."

Ginny's upper torso leaned toward me. "I'm not sure if I want to answer them. I'm still not sure how I feel about our last meeting." But then her outline stabilized and her features cleared, and she looked like the pretty young woman I knew she'd been in life. "Was the list helpful?"

"Yes, it was. And thank you for that. I really hope that you can help again, because someone's taken Clarence."

Ginny nodded, unsurprised. "You know, you're not very nice to Clarence."

My spine straightened. Sure, Clarence and I had our disagreements, our never-ending negotiations, our vastly differing opinions on topics like porn, theft, and where one should relieve oneself, but generally, I thought we managed to get along moderately well. "We make do. It's a difficult situation, but it's not like either of us has much choice."

Ginny shook her head. "That's not right. Clarence chose you."

"He was assigned to me," I corrected her gently, but still the flicker increased.

"He chose his caretaker. He chose you."

That was news to me. I thought that he'd landed with me because of my ability to communicate with ghosts. Since it was hardly a normal trait for an ex-soul collector to have, and Clarence had been assigned to me shortly after discovering that particular paranormal hiccup in my make-up, I'd assumed the two were connected—but my bosses had never actually said they were.

"Regardless of how he ended up with me, he's not in a good place, and we need to get him back."

"I like Clarence. Mostly." She bit her lip. "He should stay with someone who takes care of him and doesn't make him eat kitty kibble. With someone who rubs his belly. How do you know this place isn't better? That he doesn't get to eat whatever he wants there?"

I tamped down the urge to roll my eyes. This was about dry food and massages? The dry food kept him from completely gassing us out of the house. If he only ate his craving of the moment, which invariably included organ meat, bacon, cheese, beer, Cheetos, and vodka, I wouldn't survive the ensuing noxious fumes. And belly rubs? No. Just . . . no.

The little warning bells in my head started to clang. Those comments were very specific. "Do you know where Clarence is?"

Ginny gave me a mulish look.

She knew. She had to. Where else would she be getting the idea that his captors had given him free dietary rein? I was about sixty percent sure, maybe seventy, that Ginny knew where Clarence was being kept—or at least who had taken him.

"Bobby's pretty sure his kidnappers mean to kill Clarence—and I think Bobby's right this time," I said.

"Bobby." She huffed and flicked several ghostly strands of hair over her shoulder. "Bobby's about as clever as a cow."

It was hard to argue in favor of Bobby's vast intelligence. I bobbed and weaved that one. "Ginny, listen to me. I think maybe whoever took Clarence might have killed Bobby." I heard a gasp from the peanut gallery, but I kept my attention focused on the ghost in front of me. "If I'm right, they've killed before and won't hesitate to kill again."

I had no proof, beyond the Swiss cheese memory of a death-fugued ghost. Bobby might have been killed by random violence or someone associated with the stolen car ring he'd been involved in. Maybe he was confused, except suddenly I knew that he wasn't. I knew that what I'd said was true: the kidnappers had killed Bobby.

"No. You can't know that. Bobby had death fugue." She started to flicker. "You can't know they killed Bobby, because you don't even know who they are!" She was flickering so fast that she looked like an old, poorly preserved film. "You're lying! I *hate* liars."

Clive the gnome floated up in the air, just like the condiments she'd smashed in my kitchen. Only Clive wasn't glass —he was cast iron. And it wasn't just me in the line of fire. There were three innocent people present. I glanced at my peanut gallery and revised that to two innocent women and a somewhat shady neighborhood witch. Keeping my eyes on Ginny, I moved slowly to my left. "I'm not lying. I don't know how, but I know I'm right."

The flickering slowed just a bit. "Like a vision?"

"No." As the flickering picked up, I quickly said, "But sort of. A vision without the visuals." Sure, why not? That sounded close enough to the truth. I stepped again to my left, hoping that if I moved far enough, the ladies—witch inclusive, because even shady witches could be ladies—wouldn't be in the line of fire.

The flickering stopped, and Ginny giggled. "A vision without the visuals. You're funny, Geoff."

I took one more step to my left, relatively confident that I'd changed the angles enough to now be the singular target. So long as she kept her attention on me. "Do you think you can help me find Clarence? I truly believe he's in danger." When she still hesitated, I added, "But you're right about the food. I'll try to find something tastier for him."

Preferably something that wouldn't give him noxious gas on par with the chemical warfare of my generation. But she didn't need the details.

"Okay," she said in a cheerful tone. And I immediately felt like I'd been out-negotiated by a master. "He's with Nicky."

Not knowing what Ginny gained from this deal made me itchy. But there were bigger, more immediate problems than Ginny's unpredictable mood swings. For instance . . . "Who's

Nicky?" And had he been on our suspect list? But Ginny would hardly know that answer.

"The Gonzalez house," Sylvie called. "Mrs. Gonzalez's nephew."

"Mrs. G? Are you sure, Ginny?" But I regretted my questions immediately.

Clive came tumbling at me with remarkable speed.

25

I flinched. I yelled—probably profanity, but I was uncertain of the exact words. Generally, I looked like a bumbling idiot.

What I didn't do was duck.

Wild-eyed, I stared as Clive tumbled ass over teakettle directly toward my head. The world had slowed, and each rotation was distinct: round rump, then grinning face, then pointy hat, then round rump . . . Slow enough to see in great detail, but still speeding faster than I could dodge.

Beaned by a gnome—of all the undignified ways to die. And me having just retired back to mortality only a few weeks ago.

And then, no more than a hand's width from my eyes, he smacked into a wall. An invisible wall. A wall that couldn't be there. But a wall solid enough to produce a resounding thud when Clive made contact.

Clive looked up at me from the ground with his cheerful expression and his pipe clenched firmly between his teeth. And I said the most inane thing, the first thing that popped into my head: "Thank you, Clive."

Maybe he did bash me in the head after all, because I'd swear Clive winked at me.

"I'll take that thanks." Tamara leaned down to retrieve Clive. She lifted the statue like it weighed nothing and handed him to Sylvie. "You might like to put him back where he belongs. He's fond of his spot."

The subtext to her comments was too much for my almost-bashed-in head to process, so I ignored it. "Wait, Ginny?" I looked around the garden and found no signs of her.

"Gone," Lilac said. "Too bad they don't make mood stabilizers for ghosts. Or maybe she needs therapy? There seems to be a lot of anger going on there. Girl also has some highly conflicted emotions rolling around inside her. Toward you." She raised her eyebrows. "Toward Sylvie."

"Yes." I winced. Talking about Ginny with Clarence was one thing; this was different. Lilac didn't know her, and Ginny didn't trust strangers. Striving for vagueness but not wanting to leave Lilac with a bad impression, I said, "I'm sure she has very good reasons for the way she feels."

"I'm sure you're right. Also, I'm sorry." She gave me sheepish look. "I get why you were looking for a ghost repellant before. I'm sorry about what I said, you know, judging you for wanting them to go away. I only ever have the sense they're around. I've never seen or spoken to one before. And none of them have tried to bean me. Not yet."

"Apology accepted," I said.

Sylvie returned without Clive, her mission accomplished. "Why was it we could see and hear Ginny, but not Bobby?"

"She's much stronger than your Bobby," Tamara said, swinging her bag over her shoulder. "Hop to, folks. No telling how close of an eye Mrs. G has on this place. Mrs. G." Tamara shook her head. "I never would have thought . . ."

"Well, maybe it's her nephew," Sylvie said as she opened

the gate for us. "Although I don't suppose it could be one without the other."

"What time is it?" I had notes at the house on the Gonzalezes. If only we had time to have a look at them.

"We've got an hour and a half," Tamara replied without checking a watch or cell phone. "Not much time for planning. Your house, Geoff?"

"My house," I agreed. "I want to have a look at Nicky Gonzalez's family tree. We were interrupted before, but I think it's time to find that family connection we've been suspecting."

"I've met Mrs. G, and if she's got magic, she's hiding it deeper than I can see." Tamara's bright green eyes met mine. Those eyes didn't miss anything.

"Or hiding it in a tree out back," Sylvie said. "That's what my grandmother used to say."

Tamara stopped. We were just crossing the street, so I offered her my arm in hopes she'd continue on. She patted it and said, "I'm not so old as that," then continued across the street.

Once we were safely tucked inside my house, Tamara asked Sylvie, "What was it that your grandmother used to say?"

Sylvie shook her head, confused.

"About the tree," Lilac said. "That's an odd saying."

"Oh. It's a silly thing she used to say when I was little. She used to tell me the best place to hide secrets was in a tree out back or under a . . . rock . . . in the garden." Sylvie sank down on the nearest surface, which happened to be an armchair in my living room. "I can't believe I'd forgotten that."

"Maybe you didn't. After all, you did put that rock in your garden." Lilac shrugged. "Maybe that wasn't an accident. Maybe that was your subconscious at play."

Tamara pulled the rock out of her bag—we hadn't wanted

to leave it vulnerable, sitting on my kitchen table—and handed it back to Sylvie. "See if it's ready to give up its secrets."

Sylvie grasped the stone with both hands. "How do I do that?"

"Not a clue," Tamara replied. "I didn't know your grandmother, but you did. I'm going to be busy throwing together some protections for us, so get to it. Lilac can help you." She wagged a finger at me. "And you—you're just lucky Clive didn't want to hurt you. Ginny's intent and his weren't in agreement, or I wouldn't have been able to stop him so easily."

I hated to state the obvious, but that wink was making me a little crazy. "What intent? Clive's a ten-inch iron statue."

"If you say so." Tamara made a beeline for my kitchen table, then dumped the entire contents of her bag on the surface.

Why was I—former soul collector, a retired death, and not exactly a regular guy—the only one in the room who thought her comments about Clive were odd? The relatively normal people—relatively in Lilac's case and completely in Sylvie's—weren't giving it a second thought, so I carried on as if iron statues commonly had opinions and intent. I also sent Clive another thank you. For all I knew, the little guy could communicate telepathically.

While Tamara worked on protection charms and Sylvie and Lilac tried to pry the stone's secrets from its swirling red and green surface, I retrieved the stack of papers Clarence and I had been putting together. Work histories, credit reports, phone records, bank statements, most of which I was certain had been obtained illegally.

Flipping through, I retrieved the background check on Mrs. G and her nephew, Nicky. Or Nicolas P. Granger, as he was identified in Clarence's documents. A quick scan revealed Nicky's mother as Mrs. G's sister. So, if Tamara hadn't erred in her evaluation of Mrs. G, and she truly had no magic, that meant the juice was on Nicky's father's side of the family.

Although, now that I thought about, I wasn't sure how much good that did us. It wasn't like the aristocracy or something, where a finite set of well-catalogued families held power. Magic was slippery. It skipped and jumped around. There was also a geographic component. Different regions had different beliefs, which, some theorized, led to different kinds of magic. That left a lot of uncertainty. Then again, rumor was that witches had an eye for genealogy and a head for names, so maybe Tamara would recognize one of these names.

I scribbled down three family names, in the hopes that one would ring a bell and maybe we'd know what kind of magic was waiting for us at the other end of our meeting. Assuming we were even waiting for the meeting. For all I knew, Tamara was out there getting ready to raid Mrs. G's house.

At which point I saw explosions in my future, so I grabbed the stack of papers and the note and booked it back to the kitchen.

Lilac and Sylvie had their heads ducked together, sitting next to one another on a sofa in the living room. They didn't even notice me as I passed. Tamara looked up from a small mortar and pestle where she was grinding some mysterious concoction together.

"Is that my mortar and pestle?"

"Of course. You think I keep something heavy like that in my travel bag?" She continued to grind the coarse powder in the small stone bowl using smooth, even strokes. "I like this one. You have good taste, Geoff Todd."

"Clarence ordered it on the computer, actually. But since

you like it, I'm sure he'd want you to have it." Especially since I would never use it for edible substances again.

Her eyes twinkling, she said, "He would, would he?" But she didn't call me out on my fib. "What's that you've got?"

"Three family names attached to Nicky. His last name is Granger, but I've also got Nettles and Ainsworth."

Before I could ask Tamara if any of them sounded familiar, maybe even if one were a witch family, Sylvie called out, "Ainsworth? That's my grandmother's maiden name." She and Lilac joined us at the kitchen table, returning the rock to its spot as centerpiece. "How did Ainsworth come up?"

"Nicky's paternal grandmother's maiden name, making her your grandmother's sister, perhaps? Just a moment." I flipped through the stack of papers. "I don't have anything here on Nicky's grandmother, just her name—Prudence Ainsworth Granger."

"Oh." Sylvie frowned. When she saw us waiting for clarification, she said, "Maybe it's nothing? My grandmother's name was Constance, and her little sister who died when she was a baby was named Temperance."

"Prudence, Constance, Temperance?" Lilac asked. "That's an awfully big coincidence, given the circumstances. But your grandmother never mentioned a third sister?"

"She did, but only to say they didn't get on. I never knew her name." Sylvie touched two fingers to her temple. "Please tell me this isn't actually an inheritance dispute. I know what you said before, Geoff, but I couldn't believe it."

Everyone at the kitchen table was conspicuously silent.

Sylvie groaned. "Over a rock?"

"It's clear it's more than a rock," Tamara said. "Your grandmother imprinted such a strong signature on it that it awakened Lilac's latent psychometry talent. That's no ordinary rock."

Lilac's eyes widened. "Is that what happened?"

Tamara waved a hand at her. "Later. For now, we might know part of the reason your estranged family wants this stone, Sylvie, but we still don't know what kind of magic we'll be facing in less than an hour, or what's inside that rock."

"Well, *I* don't know," Sylvie said. "Not either of those things. I didn't even know the third sister's name. I certainly wouldn't have guessed that I have a distant cousin who wants my mysterious inheritance." Sylvie sat down across from Tamara and reached out to stroke a finger across the rock. "You'd think it would be obvious, what she'd been, what she could do. But I don't know . . . I do know she could see the dead."

Tamara's eyes lit up. "The dead? Or ghosts?"

Sylvie shrugged. "They're the same, aren't they?"

Tamara deferred to me. I supposed it was my area of expertise. "Someone who can feel, see, or hear ghosts is basically a medium," I said.

Lilac raised her hand. "Like me." Then she frowned. "But I guess I'm not a very good one, since I got the detection part without the communication."

"Later," Tamara mouthed.

"In any event," I said, "we sometimes casually refer to the dead and ghosts interchangeably, but they are different. Ghosts are a small subset of the dead. A medium's magic involves ghosts, but there are others whose magic more broadly involves the dead. And the undead."

"And creatures like the construct that attacked Lilac," Tamara said. "It was never truly alive."

"So, if Grandmother wasn't a medium, what was she?" Sylvie's gaze met mine, and I felt terrible that we were twisting precious memories of her grandmother.

"Sorcerers, necromancers, practitioners of certain magical belief systems. There are a number of possibilities."

My words certainly weren't comforting, but she wanted to know.

"Those sound scary." Sylvie's voice was firm and her tone matter-of-fact, but she definitely looked worried.

Lilac leaned closer, like a small child entranced by an especially compelling ghost story. "What I want to know is what's dead, besides a ghost? I mean, everyone knows about zombies—"

Sylvie choked.

Lilac bit her lip. "I'm sorry. And we're so short on time . . ." She settled into her seat. "I'll be quiet. Promise."

"We're no nearer to knowing what this rock does." Tamara stroked it, as if it were a living thing and needed to be placated. "If anything, we've broadened the scope of possibilities. All we know for sure is that your grandmother wanted you—not her sister's people—to have it. We can't give it away knowing nothing more. It's also unfortunate I didn't recognize any of the family names. Without some knowledge of what to expect, it's difficult to prepare for battle."

Battle? I didn't let my concern show, because neither Lilac nor Sylvie needed to see me worried. But *battle?* I was *mortal* now. Things like battles made me break out in nervous hives. Worse, Sylvie and Lilac had no business anywhere near a supernatural conflict.

"A battle is just another word for conflict, Geoff." Tamara's grass-green eyes looked into mine. "You really must learn to think quietly. But you're not wrong about these two. Lilac, Sylvie, it's for the best that you stay here while Geoff and I do what we can for Clarence."

Sylvie looked stricken. Then she stood up and stepped away from the table. "While you *do what you can*? I don't think so. You don't sound the least bit confident. And it's my rock, stone, inheritance." She gestured wildly at the rock. "I'm going with you."

"Me too." Lilac stood up and moved to stand next to Sylvie. "But, um, I just don't want to miss anything." She gave Sylvie a sheepish grin.

Sylvie nodded with a determined look. You'd have thought Lilac had just declared her unwavering devotion to the pursuit of justice for all, rather than expressing a keen fear of missing out.

"So." Sylvie placed her hands firmly on her hips. "What's next?"

Tamara gave Lilac and then Sylvie a soul-searching look with those intense eyes of hers. She must have been satisfied, because she said, "All right, then, since you're so sure."

I didn't get a second glance, let alone a soul search. Probably a good thing, because I wasn't at all sure. But Clarence needed rescuing. And it was the right thing to do.

"We're off to ask for some help," Tamara said. "Protection charms aren't my particular specialty, and we could use some good supplies." A reasonable enough plan. Being properly equipped always seemed a good choice when heading into . . . *conflict*. But then Tamara lowered the boom: "It's time to get Hector's help."

"Hector, as in the same man you told me not to disturb during daylight hours?" It was most certainly daylight. Our three hours were close to running out, but we were hours from darkness.

This wasn't sounding good. And that was without the added consideration of Hector's unknown nature. His other-than-human nature.

Lilac's eyes widened. "Heavens above and hell below. I'm meeting a vampire."

With a disapproving frown, Tamara said, "Quit that. Vampires are nasty, dirty creatures. And you'd be hard-pressed to find a *helpful* vampire." She shook her head, as if even the thought were outrageous.

Vamps tended to turn my stomach, and after the first several hundred corpses as a soul collector, that was hard to do.

"How do you think Hector, who is not a vampire"—I glanced in Lilac's direction—"can help us?"

"I think he might have a trick or two up his sleeve." Eyes twinkling with mirth, Tamara said, "Hector's a demon."

26

D emons. As in fire and hell and brimstone . . . maybe? I hadn't actually had any dealings with them. Hadn't known they were more than myth until now.

Soul collectors were kept in the dark about certain things: where collected souls were sent, whether the afterlife was indeed a better place, the existence of a heaven or a hell. Basically, anything that would impede a soul collector in his or her duty of ushering the departed on to their next stop. The existence of demons seemed to indicate certain answers to some of those questions.

"Sure, let's go visit the demon down the street. Why not?" Sylvie muttered to herself as we walked single file down the sidewalk.

Tamara's look-away spell was more likely to work when we weren't bunched together, and we didn't want Nicky and Mrs. G to know that we were going to Hector for help. One had to assume they were spying on the neighborhood, and that the sudden cooperation between the stone heiress, the witch, the medium, and retired death had put them on high alert.

And I'd also be keeping an eye on things if I was illegally searching one neighbor's house and stealing another neighbor's cat. But that was me.

Hector's house, like Tamara's, had signs of a supernatural occupant, but much subtler. I opened the gate to the front yard and felt a slight resistance as I entered the yard—except for that. I held the gate as Sylvie, then Lilac, and finally Tamara passed through, and each woman caused a ripple as she passed. Not subtle at all.

Hector had basically posted the supernatural equivalent of a security sign in the yard. In addition to the barrier around the property, Hector's yard couldn't have been more different from Tamara's. Neatly clipped grass, a fruit tree, a few blooming but magically impotent plants—pleasant, but not the yard of a person who spent much time tinkering in and with nature.

The door opened before we arrived, and the tall man I'd only briefly glimpsed the day of the explosion stood there. He didn't look particularly happy to see us.

"Are you going to invite us in or glower at us?" Tamara asked with a slightly snippy tone. Someone's harmony was out of balance again.

Hector leaned against the doorframe, relaxing slightly. "I don't know, witch. What trouble have you brought with you?" The smile he flashed first Lilac and then Sylvie was flirtatious. Not overly so, just enough to be charming, to make a woman think that she was attractive and he couldn't help noticing.

This guy was good.

Tamara pushed past Hector—and since the man was bulging with muscles, it was clear he allowed her to. "No time for your devilish ways, Hector. We might be spotted outside."

"You think whoever you're hiding from can get a look

inside my security bubble?" Hector motioned for us to come inside, tipping his head at the women as they murmured quick introductions and then offering me his hand. His shake was firm, but not challenging, and just the right length to say, "I'm self-confident, but not arrogant."

I was starting to not like this Hector guy on principle. Forget that he was a demon—whatever that meant—he was too perfect.

"I'm not talking magic, Hector. They could use binoculars. I'm worried about the neighbors." Tamara headed straight to the kitchen without hesitation or direction, so she was no stranger to his house.

Hector closed the door with a thud. "That's unfortunate. I had high hopes for the neighborhood. But given the recent direction it's taken, I suppose I'm not surprised."

"Gentrification?" I asked, wondering at the connection.

He smiled. Of course, it was perfect. "No, Geoff Todd, not gentrification." He used my name as if he found it amusing. "The fact that our quiet little street has become a supernatural hot spot. We're attracting all sorts. No offense intended. Your sort I welcome."

"Retired soul collectors." We weren't exactly a huge demographic.

"Not exactly. I find soul collectors generally fall into two categories: chaos-loving and eternal optimists. You seem the latter." He broke eye contact, turning his attention to retrieving drinks.

His evaluation, when viewed within my experience, was surprisingly astute. Surprising since his direct contact with soul collectors had to be limited. I hadn't even known demons existed, so I was either shielded from that knowledge because of a devilish connection or they were just rare.

After producing cold cans of fizzy water and inviting

everyone to sit, Hector said, "So, witchy lady, what exactly can I do for you?"

Hector really was a hard man not to like, and I wasn't seeing signs of his reported daytime moodiness.

Tamara glanced at the kitchen clock. "We've got about twenty minutes to come up with a rescue plan for Geoff's, ah, ward."

Clarence wasn't my ward—not exactly. Semantics, I supposed, but labeling Clarence as my ward made me feel all the more responsible for his welfare and therefore his kidnapping.

Sylvie popped open my fizzy water, pushing the can closer to me. Quietly, she said, "It's not your fault. If it's anyone's, it's mine for getting you involved in my family's inheritance dispute."

Hector perked up. "Family squabbles? Tamara, you should know better. That's the worst sort of trouble."

Tamara snorted. "You should know me better. It's nothing like that." As she pulled the rock from her travel bag, she said, "The Gonzalezes have kidnapped Geoff's cat."

Hector raised a brow. "You mean the cat who's not a cat?"

"That's the one," I said. "Clarence." I didn't provide a last name, but only because I didn't know it. Part and parcel with Clarence's murky history.

But Hector's full attention had moved to the rock. He reached out but stopped suddenly. "May I?" And interestingly, the question was directed to Sylvie, even though she had yet to be identified as the relevant "family" in this particular dispute.

Glancing at Tamara for confirmation first, Sylvie said, "Yes, please."

As he took the rock in his hands, that brilliant smile he'd flashed earlier reappeared. "I haven't seen one of these in a very long time."

Which made me look at him more closely. Because when he said "very long time" in his deep, appealing voice, I believed he meant a *very long* time. Years? Decades? More?

Tamara frowned. "Well, if I'd known you could decode it, I'd have brought it around earlier. We came by primarily for armaments."

We had? Right, because we were going into battle. I really hoped this talk of battle and weapons was all a huge, overextended metaphor for a more civilized conflict—if there were such a thing.

Sylvie leaned forward. "So you do know what it is?"

Hector gave her a curious look. "You don't?"

Tamara, Ms. Harmony and Light, punched him in the arm. Either she packed more of a wallop than her size indicated, or she'd put a little magic behind it, because Hector winced. Then he winked at her.

"It's a fancy box." He tipped his head. "A portable vault."

"There's something inside?" Sylvie asked, peering intently at the rock. Hector nodded, and then she asked, "Do we have to break it open?"

Hector laughed. "No. You don't have to break it. What's inside isn't a physical thing."

"Thank goodness. That would have made me feel terrible."

Hector's gaze met Sylvie's. "Exactly. And that should be enough to tell you it isn't the right course of action."

"Hm. If you think so," she said with no confidence at all.

Were Hector and Sylvie having a moment? If Clarence were here, he would probably know—or have a well-formed and incorrect opinion. Whatever was happening, it made me uncomfortable. If I was honest with myself, I was jealous. But there was also that unanswered question: what exactly was a demon? So . . . maybe I should be uncomfortable?

Either way, Clarence's clock was ticking down. "What

you're saying is that we shouldn't trade the portable vault," I asked, "because we don't know what's inside."

"You most definitely should not trade the vault, because I know what's inside." Hector held the rock between his hands, and as he replied, his voice deepened to a rumble and his eyes began to glow. "Power."

Everyone in the kitchen grew very still, even Tamara.

A collective sigh of relief swept the room when his eyes dimmed, and he said in a casual tone, "Your family gifts power through inheritance."

Inherited power? I hadn't heard of such a thing.

But then Hector set the stone down and rubbed his hands together. "I have a plan." The glint in his eye, a mischievous twinkle, not a demonic glow, made me wonder if Hector held a little love in his heart for the chaos he'd mentioned earlier. Or at least a love of conflict. That seemed a demon sort of trait.

"Are you going to share this plan," Tamara asked, "or wait for us to beg?"

"I would never make you beg, Tamara." He arched an eyebrow. "Not in these circumstances."

Which made me blink. Maybe I didn't need to worry about Hector and Sylvie. Maybe Hector's love life was fully booked.

I hoped.

Tamara crossed her arms, but there was a crinkle at the corner of her eyes that softened the gesture. "Spill already, demon."

"Do they know you have the stone? Or are you theoretically still looking for it?" Hector asked.

Given how little he knew of the situation, that seemed an awfully specific question.

"Still looking," Sylvie said. "But how did you know?"

Hector touched the rock with a finger. "Because this

power is meant for you. That you have the rock, and it's not been emptied of its gift, tells me you haven't had it for long." He pulled his attention away from the rock. "Here's what we're going to do. First schedule a trade for a neutral, but controllable location. You pick both the time and place. Also, ask for proof of life."

Sylvie paled. "Can we do that? They said they would give us instructions in twenty minutes."

"They want what we have, and what we have is unique," Tamara said. "It's a risk, but I think a good one. And it gives us more time to dig through Hector's armory."

I tried not to blink at the word *armory*, but most likely failed.

Lilac lifted her hand. "We can have the handoff at my place. It's not exactly neutral, but it's familiar to both parties." She narrowed her eyes. "Given that construct they sent after me, they certainly know about it."

"But what then?" I asked. "How do we actually get Clarence back, preferably in one piece?"

"Well, we give them exactly what they want." Hector tapped the rock again. "We just make sure Sylvie has emptied it first. And if that fails, we get our hands a little dirty."

27

Wednesday early afternoon

Getting Clarence back in one piece and getting our hands a little dirty were difficult for me to reconcile. Potentially even mutually exclusive.

Hector had confidence it could be done, but he also had less at stake. Clarence might be a hassle, he might leave noxious gases in his wake and steal my credit card with alarming frequency, but he also seemed to be hiding a few good qualities under all that fur. Maybe I'd find out what they were if he made it home.

Hector and I left the lady folk—his words, not mine—to inspect the armory. They stayed in the kitchen composing the perfect text message, while Tamara also worked on enchanting the phone. She wasn't sure persuasion would work via text, but she was willing to give it a try.

Hector opened a huge wooden door to a set of stairs and gestured for me to precede him. I walked up the stairs thinking that a basement would be a more fitting repository for what I expected to be his stash of crossbows, maces, swords, knives—

"Wow. This is amazing." The words tumbled out as I stepped into a beautiful private library.

Except it wasn't just a library.

Books lined two walls from floor to ceiling—no small task, given that the room we'd entered encompassed the entirety of the second floor of the house—but there was also an assortment of gadgets. I spun around. And pottery. Jewelry, vintage clothing . . . I wanted to spin around until I'd seen everything. No, I wanted to touch everything. Read everything.

"It's like a museum and a library." Then I spotted a massive wooden table that Hector was obviously using as a workspace. And then the reading nooks with the window seats and natural light. "A museum and library and office. It's heaven."

Hector quirked an eyebrow.

"Oh, I'm so sorry. No offense intended, just a turn of phrase," I rambled, still overwhelmed by the absolute wonder the space evoked. No, wonder held an edge, and this space was all curves. I felt at peace. Welcome.

"Now, see, I knew I liked you, Geoff." Hector's voice brought my attention back to him.

"Thank you," I said, a little surprised. Some of my earlier thoughts about him returned, and I experienced more than a twinge of guilt. "I appreciate you welcoming me into your . . ." Words failed to describe the space.

With a chuckle, he said, "Tamara refers to it as my armory. Her sense of humor isn't shared by all, but she's also not entirely wrong."

Before he could explain, Lilac trotted up the last few steps. "We did it! We got the meeting changed. It's just after dark now." Lilac's bubbling update screeched to a halt.

"Heavens above and hell below," she whispered, her eyes huge as she took in Hector's sanctuary. Then her gaze landed on him and she frowned. "Oh, sorry—"

Hector held up a hand. He waited to speak until Sylvie and Tamara joined us. Sylvie didn't have much of a chance to take in her surroundings before he began. "There seems to be some misunderstanding as to my exact nature." He glanced at Tamara, but there was no harsh judgment there. He appeared amused more than anything else. "Am I from hell? Am I the son of Satan?"

"Oh, thank the goddess," Lilac said. "I've been dying to ask."

"Lilac!" Sylvie said.

"What? We have time now. If I'm going into battle with a" —she looked around the room—"with a scholarly curator from hell, I want all the details first."

Hector's baritone laugh rumbled through the room. Once his amusement died down, he said, "The existence of heaven or of hell haven't been conclusively proven or disproven, so we'll say I'm ambiguous on the question, but I most certainly did not originate from either hypothetical place. And while my father and I have a . . . difficult relationship, I'm certain he's not Satan."

Lilac cocked her head. "But then, how are you a demon?"

"Demon is a catch-all term for a group or beings with specific types of powers." He sounded much like a father speaking to a young child: primarily patient, but with a touch of indulgent amusement and a smidge of condescension.

Not having had dealings with demons in the past, I wasn't certain if inquiring as to one's powers was considered indelicate.

Lilac didn't share my uncertainty. "So, what cool stuff can you do? I'm a medium, oh, and as of today, I can do psychometry. I think. So?"

As if revealing her own skills obligated the man to share . . .

But then Hector flashed his charming grin.

There comes a point when something is so obviously true, it's no longer an expression of subjective opinion. That point was now, and the subjective truth was that Hector was one handsome devil. Hopefully, he was too busy with Tamara to have any aspirations in Sylvie's direction.

Not that I had aspirations in Sylvie's direction.

Not exactly.

"I'm a master of the cursed object." Hector dropped that bomb like it wasn't one at all.

"What?" I snapped, then felt my neck warm. "Sorry. That sounds like a handy skill."

"Very." He let me dangle a bit, then said, "But not in the way you mean."

"Do you want me to punch you?" Tamara asked Hector. To the rest of us, she said, "Cursed is a term of art. It simply means the ability to imbue objects with self-sustaining magic."

My brain twisted that around to fit the man we'd met. "So one could use cursing as a force for good."

"Exactly," Hector replied.

Cursing for the greater good. An interesting concept, certainly.

Lilac nodded with a satisfied look on her face. "Now that's cool."

"And a PR problem," I muttered as I eyed the shelf of books nearest us. I desperately wanted to start digging through some of these books he had collected. "Demons, curses . . . a PR nightmare," I mumbled.

The walls practically shook with the sound of Hector's laughter. Since I'd been drawn in by the room's attractions and hadn't been entirely minding my words, I was caught off guard by Hector's response.

When his laughter died down, Tamara asked, "Everyone passed?"

Hector didn't respond directly, not that I could see, so I hoped the answer was yes. I still couldn't shake that "moody during daylight hours" warning Tamara had issued when she'd first mentioned Hector.

Rubbing his hands together, Hector said, "Let's talk cursed objects and rescue plans."

Turned out Hector's magic was much stronger at night, which meant the tools of his trade—objects cursed by him and managed by him in his library-armory—also worked much better at night.

My curiosity was piqued as to his other talents, but he wasn't saying, I wasn't asking, and even Lilac was silent on the subject.

It took us twenty minutes to decide on the simplest course of action: trade the rock for the cat, and if that didn't work, then run like hell with Clarence in tow. Basically. It was a little more complex than that, especially the recovering Clarence part.

In the remaining time, we—meaning Sylvie—had to pry whatever was inside that rock loose.

Two hours later and Sylvie had nothing but a headache. I still sat across the kitchen table from her. Lilac was checking in regularly, but was primarily consumed with the "toys" in Hector's library. She'd been admonished to look, not touch, and had only agreed when Hector told her he'd know if she got overly inquisitive. Tamara had left to retrieve lunch fixings, since Hector hadn't been expecting company.

Hector had remained to help Sylvie crack the rock's code. He handed her a second can of sparkling water and a bottle of painkillers.

"You're sure you can't just do this yourself? You know, use a little brute magical force and pry the thing open?" She popped two pills into her mouth and chased them with fizzy water.

Hector shook his head. "I'm surprised your grandmother didn't leave instructions. You're certain she never discussed anything that might have been a hidden message? Something to do with unlocking or revealing, maybe?"

Sylvie shrugged then rubbed her temple. "What about a key? If we need a key, then this is pointless."

Hector studied the rock. "I don't think so." But he didn't explain his reasoning.

Maybe it talked to him. He was a master of cursed objects, after all.

Hector's turn of phrase, "hidden messages," reminded me . . . "Remember when you told us about that saying, the one about hiding secrets?"

"Yes, but I don't really see how that fits," Sylvie replied.

"Did she have any other odd sayings? Bits of advice, anecdotes, funny sayings . . . anything like that?" My gut said I was onto something, but my gut wasn't very precise and hardly scientific.

"I don't know." She shook her head. "Maybe? My brain's about to explode. If this wasn't time sensitive, I'd set it aside and come back to it with fresh eyes. Who knew that thinking could be so tiring? I feel like I've been on my feet working all day." She rubbed her neck for a few seconds, and then a mingled look of excitement and chagrin crossed her face.

She had it.

"You know?" I asked. She looked hesitant. "You know. Trust yourself."

She sighed. "I might have an idea. Hector, do you have a heavy cloth? Something like denim or canvas?"

After seeing Hector's library-museum-sanctuary-office, I

was sure he did. Probably a magical version that never ripped, or one that didn't stain.

Hector retrieved a small, perfectly ordinary flannel cloth from a kitchen drawer. "Something like this?"

Sylvie accepted the cloth with a tentative smile. "I hope so."

And then she sat at the kitchen table and scrubbed on a perfectly clean rock like it was covered in grime—or, from the grim expression on her face, something much worse.

Three or four minutes passed. Her arm had to be sore.

"Can I help?" Watching her toil while I twiddled my thumbs made me uncomfortable.

"No, I don't think so." She switched the cloth to her other hand. "If I'm right, I have to do this myself."

She worked at that rock until my arms ached just watching her, periodically switching the cloth from her right hand to her left, then left to right.

And then, suddenly, she stopped. The cloth fell from her nerveless fingers.

The rock didn't glow. It didn't levitate or change colors. In fact, it looked exactly the same. But something changed. I just knew.

Sylvie's eyes grew wide, and her gaze shifted to the corner of the room. She looked so terribly sad. My eyes burned with sympathy, though hers were dry. She didn't cry, but she looked stricken.

Several seconds passed, then she collected herself and turned her attention back to Hector and I.

"It's done," Hector said.

"It is." She was more subdued than I expected. With a sad smile and a quick look to the corner of the room, she said, "The magic word isn't 'please'; it's 'elbow grease.' My grandmother used to say that when I was a little girl. I teased her that it was two words, but she would smile and say that I should work hard for the things I want, and not just ask nicely. That's how she was." A tear slipped down Sylvie's face.

She brushed it away quickly, and then took a drink from her can of fizzy water.

Hector busied himself in the kitchen, but I didn't want to leave her, not like she was, as if someone had turned the volume down or washed out the colors that were Sylvie. "Ah, do you feel any different?"

"Not really." Her gaze darted to the corner of the room. "But I'm pretty sure I can see ghosts. That, or I've overdosed on over-the-counter pain meds and am hallucinating."

"Not on two aspirin." I looked at the corner. "Do you want to talk about it?"

She shook her head then looked at the rock and frowned. "It's all so anticlimactic. I don't feel any different, nothing seems to be happening . . . except—" She gestured to the corner, the space where she'd seen her first ghost. "The rock looks exactly the same. *Feels* exactly the same."

Hector returned with a shot of some dark liquid. He saw me eyeing the fat shot glass. "Espresso."

Sylvie reached out to take the glass but then her hand hovered in the air. "Oh, it's so . . . beautiful." This time when she reached out her hand, it wasn't for the espresso.

Hector dodged her, placed the shot glass in front of her, and retreated. "Ah, no. You can't pet someone's aura."

Sylvie blushed a fiery red. "I am so sorry. I have no idea what I was thinking."

Tamara walked into the kitchen with a grocery bag that looked to be full of actual groceries. "No need for embarrassment. You were thinking what everyone thinks when they catch their first glimpse of Hector's daytime aura: that it's one of the most gorgeous things you've ever seen. Angelic, even." Tamara shared a glance with Hector that made him look decidedly uncomfortable.

Lilac arrived on Tamara's heels and craned her neck to see what was in the bag. "Wait—whose beautiful aura?"

"Hector's," Sylvie replied.

Lilac's head shot up, groceries forgotten. She scrutinized Hector—who I'd swear was blushing, except his skin was dark enough to hide it—and finally said, "No, I can't see it. I've never been able to see auras." She grinned at Hector. "But I'm not surprised yours is gorgeous."

Hector might be comfortable with his physical self, but his metaphysical self was something else entirely. And that made me wonder if this was in part the cause of his daytime grumpiness. Tamara had clearly said "daytime aura."

But I took pity on him and redirected the conversation. We were guests in the man's home, after all. "Sylvie cracked the rock—metaphorically, anyway."

"Hm. Yes, I see that." Tamara set about unloading the groceries she'd retrieved, seemingly quite at ease in Hector's kitchen. "It appears, Sylvie, that your grandmother was holding out on you. She wasn't a medium. With her power, you have all the markings of a necromantic mage. Now, who would like a sandwich?"

28

Small problem with being a necromantic mage—or anything else that was visible to the trained eye—Nicky might see the signs, just like Tamara, and know immediately that Sylvie had cracked open the family vault.

Unlike Sylvie's family, who'd been less than enchanted by their wacky, sometimes ghost-seeing grandmother and denied any connection to the supernatural world, Nicky's family seemed to have embraced magic with open (and greedy) arms.

Tamara and Sylvie had declined help preparing the sandwiches, and I suspected Tamara had used their time alone to answer some of Sylvie's questions. Whatever was said had put Sylvie more at ease. I was itching to mimic Lilac and blatantly ask—about necromantic mages and ghostly grandmothers—but unlike Lilac, I had some self-control.

It was well past lunchtime, so when the pile of sandwiches arrived, they didn't last long. Our hunger sated, we sat around the kitchen table and spitballed the best methods for shielding Sylvie's newfound powers.

Lilac asked, "Why not dig around in that magic man cave of yours, Hector, and pull out the perfect solution?"

"The concern is that Sylvie's magic, which is still new and unfamiliar, might interact unpredictably with a cursed object," Tamara explained, as if they'd not just been talking about this very issue for ten minutes.

Lilac rolled her eyes. "Like that's a greater risk than asking poor Sylvie to do the equivalent of complex math while being grilled by kidnappers and negotiating Clarence's safe return."

"What do you think, Hector?" Tamara asked. "Worse to try new magic or to try a cursed object with new magic that not's actually in play?"

"Ah, do I get a vote?" Sylvie asked. Everyone turned to her. She'd been very quiet through the discussion. "These powers you guys are talking about? They don't exist, not in any usable form. I vote cursed object, because *I can't do magic.*" Now that she had everyone's attention, she took it down a notch and, in a lighter tone, said, "Also, I vote we stop calling them 'cursed' objects."

Lilac looked intrigued. "Why cursed? Why not enchanted, ensorcelled, or even just magical? Cursed is so . . . dark." She looked at me and nodded. "You were right. Demons have a PR problem."

"We'll change what centuries of culture and myth have wrought—just for you, Lilac. Let me get right on that." Hector leaned back in his chair. "After we've retrieved the cat. And I've recatalogued my library."

I took that to mean no time soon. "So, Hector, what type of cursed object do you think might do the trick? Won't Nicky be able to see a cursed object as easily as someone's else's magic?"

Hector quirked an eyebrow at me. "Plant the curse deep enough within the fibers of the object's being and you can hide the magic from most people. Not a demon, but most others."

Lilac's eyes lit up. "So are you going to make something? Or do you have the perfect 'cursed object' in mind?"

Her blatant attempt at compliance amused him. He didn't flash his usual easy smile, but his eyes crinkled at the corners, giving him away. "No, Lilac, I will not be making something in the next few hours. It's not like ordering pizza; it takes time."

Eyes huge, Lilac sat on the edge of her seat. "So? What have you got?"

He listed a few options and watched as Lilac and Sylvie paid close attention. I couldn't help but worry that Lilac's blind enthusiasm, her outright exuberance for all things magical, might be leaving her open to harm. Sylvie's more cautious approach seemed safer.

Tamara patted my hand. "She'll be fine. She's just young, and you've forgotten what youth is like."

Quietly, I asked her, "What kind of witch can read minds?" If she was going to continue to pry inside my head, then my reservations about her own privacy were going to diminish in equal proportion.

"The kind who isn't all witch," she replied quietly. "And you're right, I shouldn't be prying. But you also need to put protections in place. You're a very open person, Geoff, which makes you a lovely man, but also very easy to read for those of us with the talent." With a concerned look, she patted my hand again and then joined the most-suitable-cursed-item debate.

The eyeglasses won in the end.

Hector handed Sylvie a pair of feminine-looking glasses. "So long as you're looking through the lenses, your magic should be hidden from view. So don't take them off." With a serious look, he added, "And don't lose them."

Tamara sighed. "Don't start with the 'cursed objects in the wild' speech."

"Since you mention it, there are several excellent points that you should all be made aware of. And it's not a speech." Except Hector was wrong. It was definitely a speech, which was especially entertaining because it conflicted with the lady-killer image I'd developed of him over the last few hours.

What I gathered from his serious, heartfelt, and very speech-like pep talk was that cursed objects could be very powerful and that sometimes they were unpredictable. We should do exactly as instructed with them, no more, no less. Only some of the items under his control were created by him. Cursed objects in general could be unpredictable, and even more so if they'd been created by a demon with morally questionable objectives.

Only trained, responsible individuals should be allowed access, and under no circumstances should we ever allow one of his toys—uh, catalogued items—to return to the wild where just anyone could use them.

"The 'wild' being anywhere that's not here or under your direct supervision?" Lilac asked. And she wasn't even poking fun. She looked quite serious.

"Basically," Hector said. "There are a few responsible curators in the state, one in Austin, but certainly cursed items shouldn't be allowed into the public domain. Everyone got it?" He looked at each of us, and one by one we agreed that we did, in fact, have it.

Hector took a little of the fun out of playing with magic toys.

And then he handed me my very own magic toy: an iron knife he retrieved from a case that contained a dozen or so knives.

I turned it over in my hands. "Wow, this looks old."

"No, it's not. It's made of iron, so it gives that appearance. And it's not cursed. If Nicky's created one construct, he could have another on hand. Iron works well against constructs, as Lilac discovered." He gave Lilac an encouraging smile

"Oh!" She perked up. "I have my gargoyle in my purse downstairs. I'll make sure to bring him back to the shop."

"Excellent choice. It certainly can't hurt to have him on hand. Gargoyles can be fierce protectors and are always good luck for the owner." Hector turned his attention to me. "Works like any knife, maybe a little sharper, maybe a little more accurate. It's slick if it gets . . . uh, wet, since it's constructed entirely of iron."

I inferred wet to mean bloody, and appreciated both the warning and his discretion. Then I realized that iron shouldn't be as sharp as any knife, and certainly not more so. And increasing accuracy meant there had to be some magic, unless Hector had put some kind of whammy on me. "Wait, I thought you said the knife wasn't cursed."

"Well, there's cursed and there's just a pinch of helpful magic." Hector winked, and then handed me an ankle sheath he pulled from under the knife case. Then he retrieved an old-fashioned key from his pocket. He removed it from his key ring and presented it to Lilac. "This is for you. Just put it in your pocket and don't lose it."

He'd just given her something he clearly carried as a personal token, and I hoped she understood its value. She opened her mouth to reply and nothing came out, then she gripped it tightly in her fist for several seconds before stuffing it in her pocket. She patted her pocket and then nodded. Maybe she did understand.

Hector paused to strap on two knives of his own, as well as a wooden stake. He saw me eyeing the sharpened implement. "Useful against more than one type of undead creature, and since we don't know what we'll be up against, it's a good precaution."

All I heard was "vampires," even though he never said the word.

My fear must have shown, because he pulled out the stake and handed it to me to inspect. The point was wickedly sharp. "I grew the tree from a tiny seed and whispered words of magic to it until it let loose of this particular limb." He flashed a devilish grin. "Those words were very sharp and pointy."

My eyebrows lifted. Not like ordering a pizza indeed. I quickly returned the stake.

He clapped me on the shoulder. "You'll be fine, but just in case . . ." He held up a finger. He left to pull a jar off the shelf furthest from the stairs. He returned and placed it on the table we'd gathered around. "A small insurance policy against infection from the dead."

Lilac thumped the table. "I knew it! Vampirism is contagious."

"Not like you mean." Tamara peered intently at Lilac. There was a warning in her eyes. "The bite of most undead will infect but not turn you. Every creature has its own methods for continuing its kind, but an undead bite will get you sick and possibly dead—not undead."

Looking slightly paler, Lilac turned to Hector. "What do we have to do?"

He unscrewed the lid of the jar and a pungent, not unpleasant aroma escaped. It was earthy, like freshly turned soil. And spicy. No, perhaps floral? Or grass. Maybe—

Tamara leaned close. "You can't parse the scents, because they're not intended to be identified."

Lilac looked at the jar like bugs might crawl out at any moment. "What do we do with it?"

"Inhale," he replied, so we all did. He passed the jar

around, and we all got a solid whiff of the multifaceted, ever-changing, impossible-to-pin-down scent.

As Hector screwed the lid back on the jar, he said to Lilac, "Nothing's foolproof, so try not to get bitten."

While Hector replaced the jar and Lilac tried not to hyperventilate, Tamara pulled several charms from her bag. They dangled on the end of thin leather cords.

As she handed them out, she said. "Protection isn't where my expertise lies, but these may have some small benefit."

Hector snorted but didn't comment. So either they were basically useless, or our friendly neighborhood witch was being excessively modest.

Sylvie received a tiny pouch that smelled suspiciously of baked goods. Lilac's charm was a little cloudy crystal. She laughed when she touched it and said, "It's a salt crystal!"

And I got a cat. I know we were out to rescue my furry housemate, but still—my protection charm was a cat?

"Thank you," I said.

But Tamara had pried into my head, or my thoughts were shouting, because she said, "Trust me."

"So anyone have a good idea of what this Nicky character looks like?" Lilac pulled out her phone and, after a few swipes, presented us with a picture from the file Clarence had put together.

"Neither of us have met him." Tamara looked to Hector for confirmation. He nodded agreement, and she said, "Only Mrs. G. Nicky doesn't come and go much. He's kept to himself since he moved in."

They both leaned in for a good look, as did I.

Sylvie nodded. "A few times."

Uh-oh, she looked really mad. And then the volcano erupted.

"How long have they lived here?" Sylvie asked with a disgusted look at Nicky's picture.

Lilac stuffed the phone back into her pocket, quietly supplying the answer: two and a half months. She must have had more than a passing look at the files.

Sylvie took the information in stride and kept right on going. "Two and a half months they've been here. I can't help wondering what other snooping they've gotten up to, non-magical things that wouldn't have triggered Tamara's alarms." She clutched the glasses in her hand, and Hector winced. "It's just so creepy to think about. They basically stalked me. Stalked me like a, a, a—"

"Deer?" Lilac supplied.

Pointing at Lilac, Sylvie nodded with terrifying enthusiasm, stabbing her finger in the air. "Like a *deer*! And probably would have kept on doing it if you hadn't shown up, Geoff. Right across the street, and you were so sweet"—not how I remembered our initial meeting, but far be it for me to interrupt a righteously angry woman's rant—"and we talked, and then Bobby, and *ohmygod*! Nicky killed Bobby. Because of the names, and the will, and the divorce, and so they found Bobby and not me, and this is all my stupid family's fault!"

She stood there, panting, looking as one does after a righteous tirade: a little high on anger, a little relieved to have let it all out, and a little tired.

The names and the divorce part were a little confusing, but the rest I basically understood. Best not to question the unclear parts, so I asked, "Do you feel better?"

She brushed a few strands of hair away from her face, straightened her back, and took a breath. "Yes, thank you, I do. Let's go get ourselves a cat."

29

Since my car was expected, I drove to Lilac's shop.

"It's not a granddad car, Lilac. It's an American-made luxury sedan that comfortably accommodates myself and my cat and, when the need arises, four of my closest partners in crime." I couldn't believe we were having this argument now.

Lilac leaned forward so that she was wedged in between Hector and I. Hector had taken the front passenger seat, since even my spacious backseat would be cramped for him. "Granddad car. Do we need to take a poll?"

Hector and Tamara both raised their hands, which made Lilac squeal in victory. Maybe this was how she relieved stress.

I glanced in the rearview mirror at one supporter. "Thank you, Sylvie."

Her eyebrows lifted. "I'm abstaining."

And the results were conclusive: I drove a granddad car. Cars were expensive, and new cars doubly so. I wasn't getting a new one, so I gave up and shrugged. "I like it. It's a nice car."

"It is a nice car." Hector nodded amicably. "A smooth ride, plenty of legroom—but definitely a grandpa car."

No doubt Hector's car made a statement, but quietly. Nothing flashy, but definitely cool.

Sylvie's eyes crinkled, and her lips quirked with a suppressed smile. "It's okay, Geoff. If anyone can pull off a grandpa car, it's you."

When I pulled into the strip mall where Lilac's store was located, everyone fell silent. We'd arrived at the shop well in advance of the allocated time. The lights were on, and the shop sign was flipped to Open.

My concern must have shown, because Lilac leaned forward again. "I have two part-time employees that usually man the store when I have readings, need to do paperwork, or just can't come in."

Lilac, with her green hair, her lip piercing, her ghosts, and her abundant enthusiasm, was an adult who owned her own business. It was easy to forget. I'd assumed the store had been closed while she was helping us.

"Just a second." She leaned on the console between the two front seats. "They should be coming out any minute. Phoebe's closing early today, and I had her invite her boyfriend to tag along for the day."

"That's"—*odd*, but I opted for a gentler alternative—"generous of you."

Lilac snorted and pointed. "Not even a little."

A small giant dressed in khakis and a T-shirt emerged from the store, followed by a petite girl with shockingly pink hair. The pink-haired girl locked up and then the two got in the giant's truck and left.

"Perhaps not a match for a construct," Hector said, "but yes, I can see how he'd be useful generally as a deterrent."

"Yeah. She really needs the money, and I hated to close the shop for an entire day." Lilac huffed out a breath. "I made her promise if any big, scary-looking guys came in the shop and asked odd questions, she and Neil were to leave immediately, not worry about the shop, and call me after they'd left. I didn't really know the right answer, you know? This job pays Phoebe's rent. Look, are we gonna dissect my poor life choices or go in already?"

Sylvie gave her a quick one-armed hug, then exited the car, the rest of us a split second behind her. Tamara gave us a thumbs-up before disappearing around the corner. She was going to enter from the rear of the building.

"Any sign that they've showed up early?" I asked Hector.

"I have no idea, but I recommend you search the shop once inside." Hector's reply didn't fill me with confidence.

Didn't we have some kind of magical way to detect this guy? Or maybe that was Tamara's job. If so, she needed to hurry up.

Lilac unlocked the store door and tried to hold it open for us, but Hector ushered first her then Sylvie inside.

Holding the door wide for me, Hector said, "Remember, you're just here to have a conversation." Then he disappeared. Not literally. He went around back to join Tamara. But he was stealthy for a big guy.

I went inside, letting the door swing shut behind me. A conversation. Right.

We'd never given up on actually negotiating Clarence's release. It was more a question of what to do if—when— those negotiations broke down because Nicky discovered the vault had been opened. Or because he had as much anger toward Sylvie as a desire for her inheritance. Or because he'd already killed Clarence. There were so many ways it could all go wrong.

"Nicky?" Sylvie cried out as a dark-headed man stepped out of the bathroom.

He was older than the picture we'd seen. Well into his

thirties. It was a passing thought, because most of my attention was on the gun he was holding.

The gun pointed at Sylvie.

"Did you think you and your little gang were the only ones who'd come early?" Other than a slightly breathless quality, his tone was confident. The gun in his hand, however, wasn't very steady.

The answer to his question was no, we had not thought we'd be the only early ones. I didn't think he'd be quite *this* early. Then there was the fact that the shop had been open when we'd arrived, so he'd done something to convince Phoebe and her hulking boyfriend that he'd left when he hadn't. Or he'd snuck in. All things that weren't really relevant, because the gun was still pointed at Sylvie.

"Where's Clarence, Nicky?" I asked, moving away from Sylvie and Lilac while glancing behind Nicky to the back of the shop, where I hoped Tamara and Hector would triumphantly emerge and save us all.

Except they didn't. Just my luck, Nicky boy probably had a construct floating around in the alley.

The tip of the gun wavered in my direction then returned to Sylvie. "It's Nick, you arrogant ass. And Clarence is safe. You'll get him back once I have the stone."

Liar, liar, pants on fire.

Bobby? So far from—Oh, I was an idiot. He was haunting Sylvie, not Sylvie's house. I tuned out Bobby's annoying chant as best I could. Nick's armpits were damp with sweat, and the longer he held that gun aloft, the less steady it would be. I didn't actually have time to be *incredibly* annoyed by Bobby.

He was annoying beyond belief, but he did provide a great distraction in one sense. Hoping I wasn't about to get myself shot, I asked, "Why did you have to hurt Bobby, Nick?"

Confusion clouded his features. "Bobby? What does he have to do with any of this?" Which made me think my gut had been wrong, until he added, "That was weeks ago."

Yeah. He'd killed Bobby. Probably with the same gun he held in his hand now. The one whose muzzle was drifting slowly away from Sylvie and Lilac. Thank goodness.

Kill Bobby. Kill Sylvie. Then Bobby wailed, that terrible sound of grief I'd heard from him before.

Sylvie's gasp of outrage brought Nick's attention and his gun back to her, and my small gain was lost.

"You. With your suburban life and your filthy rich parents and all your advantages. Couldn't you just give us this one thing? Magic was ours! She should have given it to us!" Sweat streamed down Nick's face. "When my gran was dying, she told us about her sister and you. About the power."

Something more than just stress was going on here. Nick's face looked waxy, like he was ill. Maybe on drugs.

"You *killed* my ex-husband! For what?" Sylvie pulled the rock from her bag. "This?"

I sent up a prayer of thanks that Nick hadn't shot her when she reached for it. Apparently, Lilac had similar feelings, because she clasped her hands together and looked heavenward.

Just as I was certain Sylvie was going to chuck the rock at his head and still end up shot, a sharp thud reverberated through the small shop.

Bobby's wailing stopped, and everyone flinched—but not Nick. If he had, with that gun in his twitchy hands—

Another thud, this one even louder, had us ducking—but not Nick.

After the third thud, I traced the sound to its original: a construct pounding on the glass door.

He was larger than the first construct and highly motivated to get inside. So motivated that, with his supernaturally enhanced strength, he should have shattered the glass door.

The construct's bulk and awkwardness would have been harder to sneak past Phoebe, certainly, but I was surprised Nick didn't simply kill Phoebe and her beau, leaving the place empty. Why hadn't we been confronted with Nick, his construct, and two more victims?

But then the creature's eyes glowed a dim purple color. Glowing eyes . . . I looked at Nick and saw the sweat, pallor, and shakiness for what it was. Exhaustion. He was directly controlling the construct. That wasn't how they worked; they weren't puppets. Which was why Nick was killing himself with the effort.

"Why can't it get in?" Nick glared at me, and for the first time, the gun was nowhere near Sylvie. "What did you do, reaper?"

Lock. Lock-lock. A manic, high-pitched giggle followed.

"Soul collector," I said. "No scythes required." It was an automatic response to the age-old slur, not because I wanted to get shot, but because my brain was busy trying to figure out why that construct couldn't get in. Hector and Tamara weren't likely to be the cause. They'd have joined us by now if they hadn't found their own trouble.

"Soul collector, reaper, death, why can't it get in?" Nick was desperate. Sweat was streaming off him.

But why? Why was he so frantic? He was the man with the gun.

In the background, Bobby kept chirping, *Lock*.

Finally, that piece clicked into place. Lock, lock and key. The key in Lilac's pocket. We were locked in this store, safe from outside harm. That had to be what was keeping the construct out. And I trusted Hector's cursed objects. That construct wasn't getting in.

But why was Nick literally killing himself to get the creature inside?

And I looked at him. Not in a panic, not while trying to talk him down or draw his attention away from Sylvie. I just looked. His eyes were wild, his hair soaked, his skin waxen— and his finger was on the trigger guard.

"Nick." He didn't hear me, so I repeated his name twice.

Finally, he looked at me. His eyes weren't wild, but tired and confused. "Why can't it get in?"

"A demon's cursed object is protecting the shop. No one, nothing, is getting inside." I saw Lilac pat her pocket and then practically collapse with relief.

Sylvie, on the other hand, was eyeing the gun, then Nick, then the gun. I wasn't convinced she'd keep her cool. She looked mad enough to grab the gun from Nick, and that might be just enough push for him to actually get the gumption to shoot her.

Nick's legs wobbled, and he leaned against the edge of Lilac's desk. The tip of the gun was pointing away from us, toward the ceiling, wavering. I had a nasty feeling. A choking, breath-stealing feeling.

"Nick." I tried to sound calm. I tried.

The tip of the gun rested against his head, the muzzle still pointed at the ceiling. "I saw the opportunity. With your cat." His gaze met mine briefly then shifted away. "I knew it wasn't a cat. Knew he was alone in the house. It was easy. He asked if I had good food and then he just came with me." Nick shrugged. "Easy."

"Nick, give me the gun." Again, I spoke calmly. No accusations. Simple instructions. Focusing on what I wanted him to do.

But he ignored me. Tears appeared in his eyes. "Bobby. Now that shouldn't have happened. I just wanted to know where you were. The will and your name change . . . I couldn't find you." He tried to make eye contact with Sylvie, but I stepped to the side, intercepting him and keeping as much of his focus on me as possible. Looking at me now, he said, "Her name was different. On the will, she had his name."

"Bobby's name."

"Yeah." He looked at me like I'd just admitted to understanding everything. "Exactly. So I found him."

"But he wouldn't help you," I said in a neutral tone. But it was hard, because a few of Bobby's pieces were falling into place, and it made my head and my heart hurt. He'd died protecting his ex-wife and then he'd stayed, as much of him as had survived, to make sure she was safe.

All of this—Bobby's death, stalking Sylvie, hurting Lilac, Clarence—for one man's greed.

"You sorry son of a—" Sylvie stopped abruptly, and I heard Lilac making shushing noises. I hoped Lilac had the sense to physically restrain Sylvie.

I kept my eyes on Nick, on the gun. "Nick, give me the gun."

And then he did.

He just handed it to me.

I dropped the clip into my hand, pocketed it, cleared the chamber, and then almost passed out.

Thankfully, Hector and Tamara waltzed through the back door, Mrs. G in tow, at exactly that moment.

I couldn't pass out in front of a woman I had romantic interest in, a guy who had both the coolest toys and the most enviable playhouse, and two women who would never let me forget.

Except maybe I could.

Sylvie appeared from nowhere and wrapped an arm around me. Okay, she propped me up. Either way, I stayed on my feet and didn't pass out.

30

When I'd finally caught my breath and was sure I wasn't going to embarrass myself with a quick trip to the ground, I leaned down and whispered a thank you in Sylvie's ear.

She leaned in, gave me a quick, one-armed squeeze, then let me go. And I felt like a heel. She'd just confronted her burglar and her husband's murderer, and she was making sure I didn't hit the pavement with a splat.

I redirected those feelings toward a smug demon and his witchy buddy. "Where have you guys been?"

"It's been five minutes." Hector smacked me on the back. "I knew you were good for five minutes."

Tamara shot Hector an exasperated look. "And Mrs. G said there was no way Nick would shoot. He's terrified of being haunted. Thinks if the constructs kill for him, the ghosts can't find him."

He might be right if Bobby was any indication, but I still thought that was death fugue. "Bobby?" I called out. But there was no response. Where was he? "Has anyone seen Bobby? Uh, heard him, felt him, anything?"

But no one had.

While I'd been, ah, getting my bearings again, Mrs. G had gone to sit next to her nephew. No one had put him in cuffs —although I didn't suppose we had any—but he didn't look like he was going anywhere. He didn't look quite awake. I peered closer. He didn't look quite alive.

Tamara approached me. "He's gone." Seeing my confusion, she said, "There were two constructs in the alley. One attempted to enter through the rear door." She shrugged. "The other kept us busy without getting too close. That's what took us so long. The creature avoided a direct confrontation."

Her words made it clear who'd come out on top *every time* in that confrontation. She and Hector were maybe a little scary as a pair.

"So you were distracted by one construct, while the other tried and failed to get in, because of Hector's key," I said. "I figured the key out at some point."

Tamara rolled her eyes. "I told him to tell you, but he didn't want you relying on it. He wasn't sure it would be as effective, since she leased the space, but he's overly conservative with his precious cursed objects."

Three constructs. That was a lot of magic. A lot. "Wait. Was he controlling the two in the back directly?"

Tamara pinched her lips together. "Creativity is one thing; twisting magic to be used in ways it's not intended is simply foolish. And dangerous."

So, yes. I looked at the blank expression on Nick's face. "Are you telling me he's blown a fuse?"

"Magically speaking, yes. I don't think there's any recovering from that."

A knot of dread landed in my stomach. "Clarence."

Tamara frowned. "He wasn't in either of their cars." She

looked at Mrs. G. She was huddled next to Nick on the sofa, the same one that had propped up the construct for his blessed-water dousing and had eventually been covered with that creature's ashes. They must have moved him while I'd been speaking with Tamara.

"He's at the house." Mrs. G said in a tired, small voice. She blinked red-rimmed, dark-circled eyes at us. "The key's under the yellow flower pot." Then she turned to Nick and tucked his head against her bosom like one might do with a small child.

I felt for her. She'd been caught between the love she felt for her nephew and what she, as a good and decent person, knew was right. She'd have to live with her choices.

But those thoughts were secondary as we piled into the car to rescue Clarence. Hector, bless his efficient soul, was handling the remaining necessities with Nick and Mrs. G.

It was only as we raced back home that I realized not one of us had thought to ask if Clarence was alive.

When we entered the house, a low moaning noise greeted us. It seemed to come from the back of the house. Were we too late? Was Clarence even now in the throes of some horrible death?

"If he was dead, we wouldn't hear anything. If he was dying, we'd hear more. Don't you think?" Tamara shooed me toward the back of the house. "Go. See what's happening."

Not dead—but dying? Tortured?

The moaning got louder, and I pinpointed the room it was originating from. I could hear Tamara opening and closing doors—searching for another construct, perhaps. Or just making certain we wouldn't be surprised by anything else nasty that Nicky had left behind.

Sylvie and Lilac were both at my back, following closely.

"If the layout is as close to my house as it seems, then this is the master bedroom," Sylvie said as she gestured to the last door.

I nodded and opened it. And there he was, a pitiful, tortured bundle of fur, lying prone on his side, a look of anguish on his face.

"Save me, Geoff," he whispered.

And that was when I heard the porn tunes in the background.

A huge screen showcased a film with too much bare flesh and bad background music. I grabbed the remote on the bed and shut it off while Clarence writhed in agony.

"Clarence, what did they do to you?" I asked. I was confused, concerned . . . confused.

"Beer and brats. So many brats." He moaned again.

"And porn," Lilac said helpfully in a chipper voice.

Clarence groaned. "So much bad porn." He lifted his head slightly and looked at her. "I couldn't say no."

Sylvie's lips twitched. "Clarence." There was sympathy there, but also a laugh that I could tell wanted to burble to the surface. Thank goodness she could laugh. She'd had a doozy of a day.

"Go on, laugh." He writhed on the bed and groaned again. "But get me some kitty Pepto, pleeeeease."

His stomach was distended under all his fluffy stomach fur, which I could see more clearly now that he'd stretched out and was still. Still except for the panting. That couldn't be good.

"I think we need to get you to the vet, Clarence. You really don't look so good." I turned to grab the corner of the bedspread and caught a shared glance between Clarence and Sylvie.

Sylvie put her hand on my arm. "Don't worry, Geoff. He'll be fine. There's an emergency vet right around the corner. A friend has used them and says they're great."

"Got it. Emergency vet it is," I said as I wrapped Clarence in the bedspread. When I picked him up, the moaning increased in both volume and frequency, which made me hope that Sylvie was right. How terrible would it be for Clarence to survive the kidnappers only to be brought down by beer, brats, and porn?

EPILOGUE

Late night

Several hundred dollars later, Clarence and I were back from the emergency vet. It had been a close call. Not a medical one—Clarence was just fine—but a logistical one.

So far, everyone had believed me when I said, "Bobcat? Of course he's not a bobcat. He's a pixie bob." And if they commented on his size, which was much greater than any pixie bob, I just claimed there was a little Maine coon thrown in.

That hadn't worked at the emergency vet. It wasn't the vet who'd commented, but the vet tech. "Sir, that's a bobcat. I can see clear as day that it's a bobcat."

Clarence's eyes had narrowed, and if he hadn't been in gastric distress, I was pretty sure the tech would have gotten a nice claw to the nose.

People saw what they wanted to see, and they didn't want to see magic or the unexpected. Give them a reasonable alternative, and most people would latch on and cling to it desperately rather than deal with the idea of magic or the supernatural.

But not Horace Messerschmidt.

My guess: Horace had a little magic tucked away in his family tree. Or he was just that guy. The one who knew everything. The one who was never wrong. The one who had to tell you all about the right way to do it.

"I might want to strangle you, Clarence. First, that terrible Messerschmidt man with his lectures on having wild animals as pets, and then the bill. Seven hundred dollars." When he didn't look chastened and didn't reply, I repeated, "Seven hundred dollars, Clarence."

"Hm. I've never had an ultrasound before." Clarence sniggered. "Like a pregnant lady." Then he chuckled.

"Are you twelve?" Although that wasn't fair, because twelve seemed a little young for someone with a porn fascination. I could only hope he'd gotten *that* out of his system while locked up with Nick and his aunt.

A knock at the door precluded a response, but I gave him a look that said this conversation was not over. I answered the door to find Sylvie on my doorstep.

"I saw you were home and that the lights were still on. I just wanted to see how everything went at the vet's office." She lifted a basket. "For Clarence."

I gestured for her to come inside. She hesitated, but then nodded.

Clarence stretched and then began a slow saunter to his bedroom. "Hi, Sylvie. Excuse me while I sleep off my bender. I gotta get some shut-eye, or I'm a gonna be a cranky kitty." He gave me some side-eye, and I knew he was thinking he'd avoided our little heart-to-heart about pornography, alcohol, and gluttony—oh, and wandering away with any murderous stranger who invited you for beer and brats.

Sylvie indicated the basket she'd brought. "I'll leave this in the kitchen for you."

"Oh, that's for me?" Clarence scanned the basket. I'd swear his eyes lit up at the little stuffed mouse and the kitty grass, but he retrieved the DVD. "Thanks!" He had to speak around the DVD clenched in his mouth, but his enthusiasm was unmistakable.

He also hotfooted it to his room much faster than my seven-hundred-dollar vet bill would have indicated possible.

Sylvie watched him go with a conflicted look. "I guess he's feeling better. Wait, can he operate a disc player on his own?"

"He can type, use the phone—including programming my new cell phone—and open doors. I think it's safe to say he can manage it." Except we didn't have a player for those discs, so he was likely thieving my laptop right now to watch it. Sylvie looked guilty enough, so I kept that tidbit to myself. "What movie did you bring him?"

That brought a smile to her face. "*My Fair Lady.* I loved that movie as a child. I don't know if he'll like it, but I thought I'd give it a try. Anything to get him interested in something besides bare breasts."

"Agreed, and thank you." I took the basket from her and headed to the kitchen. "Kitty grass?" It was a bright green and a few inches tall.

She shrugged, looking sheepish. "I couldn't exactly go to bed, you know, not knowing…" She shook her head, then licked her lips. "I squeezed in at the big-box store just a few minutes before they were closing. I asked the lady at the pet store, who was a little put out. I told her it was a get-well basket, and she started to grab these things from the shelves. So I just went with it. The DVD I already had."

"Can I get you a glass of wine?" I saw she was going to decline, and quickly added, "I'd like the company. Please."

Lips pressed together, she nodded. "If you haven't talked to Tamara, then you won't know—Nicky's been hospitalized. She thinks they'll poke around for a while and eventually put him into care when they can't figure out what's wrong with him."

She seemed to prefer red, so I retrieved a bottle of my favorite red and two glasses. "I feel a little bad for Mrs. G, being placed in that situation, but—"

"She's moving." Sylvie cleared her throat, turning slightly pink. "I suggested this might not be the best neighborhood for her, given the role she played in events."

"That's best for everyone, Sylvie, even Mrs. G. You did the right thing speaking up."

As I opened the bottle, she settled herself at the kitchen table. She looked uncomfortable, ill at ease in a way that I'd not seen before. Sylvie normally glowed with a mellow cheerfulness that I found endearing, and I missed that.

Picking up a glass, I started to pour. "This wasn't your fault." Since she wouldn't meet my eyes, I figured I might have hit the nail on the head. Unless . . . "Or maybe you think Clarence and I—"

"No! Poor Clarence." Then she grinned. "Although it was a little funny to find him in that state after expecting just about *anything* else." She chuckled, caught my eye, and then broke into a belly-deep laugh along with me.

When our amusement had died down to intermittent chuckles, we sipped our wine and shared what I thought was a rather companionable silence.

But perhaps not, because when Sylvie did speak, it wasn't of companionable things. "You know it was my fault. If not mine directly, then my family's."

"I'm not sure I'd claim Nick as family. Or even Mrs. G. She was wrapped up in events that I suspect spiraled out of control. Under normal circumstances, she's probably not a person to make those choices."

"I'm sure you're not wrong. Although"—her nostrils flared as she toyed with her wine glass—"she probably befriended me in pursuit of that stupid rock. Either way, she and I both will be happier if she's living across town." She took a sip of wine. "As to family, Geoff, whatever you say, you can't actually pick and choose them. They are or they aren't."

"Not very happy with your grandmother right now, are you?"

She looked up from her wine glass, and there was anger on her face. "No. No I'm not. How could she keep that from me? Not prepare me or tell me anything about our history." She drew a deep breath. "And don't get me started on my parents. If denial were a disease, they'd be eaten up with it." Her eyes widened suddenly, and she covered her face. "Ugh. What a terrible thing to say."

"First, cut your grandmother some slack. From everything I can tell, you adored her and she adored you. Don't let what's happened in the last few days change that. And remember, you were just a child when she died. Whatever power your family has, there's probably a reason the bulk is passed through inheritance. Maybe it's simply too much for a child. Maybe it needs to be given to the right person at the right time."

She sighed. "Rationally, I know these things. But I'm mad. Knowing her, she probably wanted me to have as normal a childhood as possible. I did adore her." A sad smile tugged at her lips.

"As for your parents—"

She interrupted me with a groan, and I couldn't help a tug of sympathy at the sound.

"Yeah, a lot of people feel that way. But give them a break.

Most people are doing the best they can. Maybe not every-one, but most." I thought of my own parents, long gone, and knew in my heart that they'd done the best they could.

"Hector was right. You are an eternal optimist."

"Be that as it may, I find most people turn a willfully blind eye to the wonders of the world when those wonders are touched by magic." I leaned forward and touched her very gently on the forehead. "Consider yourself officially inducted into the special club. Now you have the ability to see. And that's thanks to your grandmother."

She grinned at my silliness and her dimple peeked out. "So you don't blame me for your friend's abduction or being pulled into a mess of explosions and family inheritance disputes?"

"One explosion, but not in the least. In fact, I was rather hoping that you would help me with a mess of my own." I looked around. "Can you tell if we're alone? You know . . ." I pointed to the corners of the room, where ghosts seemed to enjoy lurking.

"Oh." She straightened in her seat. "Yes, I think I can do that. And I think it's okay. What mess are we talking about?"

"Ah, so 'mess' isn't quite a fair description. Mystery, perhaps? Genevieve Weber was murdered here in the neigh-borhood back in the seventies."

She frowned at me. "Genevieve . . ." Her eyes widened. She hunched closer and lowered her voice. "Ginny?"

I nodded. "There's something terribly wrong about the whole thing. Her death was misidentified as a suicide, her soul collection wasn't entirely to protocol, and she came back. I didn't even know souls that had crossed *could* come back. But regardless, it's all quite unusual."

"That does sound like a mystery." Sylvie considered for a few seconds. "I'm in, on one condition. You, Geoff Todd, have to tell me all about dating back in your day."

"Ah . . ." Words failed me and my neck warmed. Ridiculous, because it was a simple enough trade. "Dating, ah, courting, yes, I can do that. Any particular reason?"

"Oh, no. None at all," Sylvie said with a mischievous twinkle in her eye.

Keep reading for an excerpt from A Date with Death, *Clarence and Geoff's next adventure!*

EXCERPT: A DATE WITH DEATH

The modern world confused me on an almost daily basis. I'd been raised in a different time. Literally. I'd been recruited in my forties to be a soul collector (one of the deaths) back in the early 1940s. Deaths didn't age during their service, because we weren't fully mortal while we served.

But I'd retired, regained my mortality, and been dropped into another century. I might have experienced the passing of time, but I hadn't *lived* it. So some of the mores of modern life I'd absorbed and others eluded me.

Enter Clarence, my ward—or roommate, given the trend our relationship was following. He'd began as an assignment. My bosses didn't know how Clarence had ended as he had, a human ghost in the physical body of a wildcat, or they weren't sharing that information with me.

He was unique in the landscape of paranormal beings. Most ghosts didn't linger long in this world, and those that did certainly weren't possessing a body. And on top of that bundle of oddness, I personally had never heard of human ghost inhabiting the body of animal. Clarence was a conundrum.

No one knew what to do with him, only that his mischievous, clever self couldn't be allowed to wreak havoc on the unsuspecting human world. Hence my very vague assignment: keep an eye on him and keep him out of trouble.

I'd only recently learned Clarence was the singular soul inhabiting the bobcat's body. He must have possessed the creature at or near its natural death. Learning that had shifted our relationship, because up to that point, I'd believed that a confused and helpless animal's conscience had been trapped inside a body it could no longer control. That belief had heavily shaded my interactions with Clarence. That and his unfathomable taste in movies.

My relationship with Clarence had a rocky beginning, but it was moving in a very different direction. He was more in tune with the world of today and had become my sounding board for all things modern. I wouldn't follow his lead blindly, but in this case his experience with modern women (sadly) outweighed my own.

"Trust me, Geoff, Sylvie was giving you the go-ahead to ask her out." Clarence perched on a kitchen chair like it was a throne. The cushion that elevated him several inches added to the royal image.

"That's not what she said. It sounded more like a historical inquiry. She asked about how people back in my day used to date. It seemed more anthropological than romantic."

"For a clever guy, you're not very smart. That was your in." He shook his head in disgust, which produced a tinkling sound. He stilled and flattened his tufted ears. "I'm not saying another word until you take this f—"

"Watch your language, or it's definitely not coming off." The battle with his language didn't seem to be following the same trajectory as his movie tastes. He remained as vulgar as ever, but that was all right. I'd persist and he'd cave…probably.

A peevish look crossed his face, but he cleared his throat and continued more civilly. "If you would please remove the *flipping* bell, I'll decode the lady-speak for you."

Light-footed, sneaky Clarence with no bell. The idea didn't appeal.

I mentioned in passing to a neighbor—not Sylvie, one who believed Clarence was a very large, very densely coated Maine Coon-Pixie-Bob cross and not a wild bobcat—that I was having difficulty keeping up with my kitty. I was especially upset at the time, because earlier that day Clarence had snuck out the front door when I wasn't paying attention and done a walkabout in the neighborhood. He'd been gone for over two hours while I searched the streets for a dead or injured body—his or someone else's. One never knew with Clarence. When I'd given up and come home, he'd waltzed through the front door minutes later as if nothing untoward had happened.

The neighbor had recommended a bell to help keep track of Clarence's movements, and I'd thought it a stellar idea.

"Actually, the bell and the collar. It's"—he narrowed his eyes—"*flipping* uncomfortable. Itches like you wouldn't believe." He cocked a hip and began to scratch his neck with feline fervor.

"Promise you won't leave the house without me."

He stopped scratching, but his eyes resumed their peevish squint. After several seconds, he said, "Agreed."

"The collar goes back on if there's any hint you've set foot beyond the yard."

He immediately perked up. "So I have yard privileges back again?"

"If you're willing to help me."

"Done," he said quickly.

"And," I continued, "you promise not to pee anywhere except outside or in *your* toilet in *your* bathroom."

His ears flattened again and his eyes squinted to narrow slits. When I didn't relent, he said in a whiny voice, "But your bathroom smells nicer."

I crossed my arms and waited.

"Fine. I'll help you. Now take this da—uh, *dang* collar off me." As soon as I'd removed the offending article, he clawed at his neck.

"Do you feel better?" I asked after watching him pitch a prolonged feline fit.

The scratching stopped as abruptly as it had begun. He sat calmly on his haunches, staring at me with a smirk plastered across his mug. "When I say that Sylvie was giving you an in, I mean that she moved the conversation in a direction that would have allowed you to then ask her on a date."

"Oh." I thought back to the moment in question. Yes, I could see how that might be the case. "But what do I do now? It's been a while."

Clarence sighed. "You man up, Geoff, and you call the woman and ask her on a date. You own your idiocy in missing the opportunity and hope that she's still interested. How am I the one who knows this?"

I ignored the question, because wasn't that obvious? Modern women were a mystery. Instead, I eyed him critically and said, "If you're sure." It had been weeks since that conversation, and I'd barely seen her. She'd been busy clearing her yard—her shed had been bombed not so long ago—and had also been working at her hair salon more than usual. "I haven't seen much of her since. If she was interested, wouldn't I have seen more of her?"

"I know you haven't. And no, you wouldn't see much of her if she thought you'd blown her off. Besides, Sylvie is one hot...uh, very attractive lady. And she's nice." He smirked. "And she likes me, so she's got great taste."

"She's perfect in so many ways, but I suppose everyone has a flaw or two."

And she was perfect, including—not in spite of—her affection for Clarence. Sylvie was a lovely woman, and I'd be a lucky devil to get that date. It was worth it, even if I was as awkward as a man who'd been out of the social whirl for over seventy years was bound to be.

"Call her, you idiot." Clarence gave me a wide-eyed look of feline innocence. "Call her, or I might decide to spray your favorite pillow the next time you leave the house, because any idiot who lets that woman get away deserves a stinky pillow."

"You know what happens if you spray anything in the house again." I tapped the collar on the table, and the bell tinkled a cheery reminder. But he was right. If I wanted to pursue a potential relationship, I had to start somewhere. "Fine. I'll call her."

"Now, Geoff. Call her now."

Nerves fluttering worse than my first soul collection, I pulled out my cell and did exactly that.

Pick up your copy of A Date with Death *to keep reading!*

BONUS CONTENT

Sign up for my newsletter to receive release announcements, bonus materials, and a sampling of my different series. Sign up at www.CateLawley.com.

ABOUT THE AUTHOR

Cate Lawley writes humorous, action-filled mysteries that frequently contain a paranormal twist.

When Cate's not tapping away at her keyboard or in deep contemplation of her next fanciful writing project, she's sweeping up hairy dust bunnies and watching British mysteries.

Cate is from Austin, Texas (where many of her stories take place) but has recently migrated north to Boise, Idaho, where soup season (her favorite time of year) lasts more than two weeks.

She's worked as an attorney, a dog trainer, and in various other positions, but writer is the hands-down winner. She's thankful readers keep reading, so she can keep writing!